The near accident with the car had left Betsy with more than a few scrapes and scratches. Her skin prickled in fear at the thought that she'd almost been run over.

She'd never felt that scared before, and she hoped she never would again. Her inability to respond to the immediate danger baffled her. Why hadn't she jumped out of the way instead of standing in the street like a frightened animal, not knowing which way to turn? If it hadn't been for Mark, she might be dead now.

She stopped at the door of Mark's car and stared back at him. No matter what she thought about Mark on a personal level, she had to admit his law enforcement training had served him well. He had reacted like a trained professional, and she owed him a debt of gratitude. Maybe her gratitude would help her overcome the hurt he'd inflicted on her in the past. Then again, maybe nothing could change how she felt. Only time would tell.

Books by Sandra Robbins

Love Inspired Suspense

Final Warning
Mountain Peril
Yuletide Defender
Dangerous Reunion
Shattered Identity
Fatal Disclosure

SANDRA ROBBINS,

a former teacher and principal in the Tennessee public schools, is a full-time writer for the Christian market. She is married to her college sweetheart, and they have four children and five grandchildren. As a child, Sandra accepted Jesus as her Savior and has depended on Him to guide her throughout her life.

While working as a principal, Sandra came in contact with many individuals who were so burdened with problems that they found it difficult to function in their everyday lives. Her writing ministry grew out of the need for hope that she saw in the lives of those around her.

It is her prayer that God will use her words to plant seeds of hope in the lives of her readers. Her greatest desire is that many will come to know the peace she draws from her life verse, Isaiah 40:31. "But those who hope in the Lord will renew their strength. They will soar on wings like eagles; they will run and not grow weary; they will walk and not be faint."

FATAL
DISCLOSURE

SANDRA ROBBINS

Love Inspired

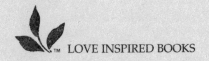

LOVE INSPIRED BOOKS

Recycling programs for this product may not exist in your area.

ISBN-13: 978-0-373-67512-8

FATAL DISCLOSURE

www.LoveInspiredBooks.com

Printed in U.S.A.

Thou wilt keep him in perfect peace,
whose mind is stayed on thee: because he
trusteth in thee. Trust ye in the Lord forever:
for in the Lord Jehovah is everlasting strength.
—*Isaiah* 26:3–4

To my family,
whose encouragement keeps me writing

ONE

A shriek much like the distress cry of a black-crowned night heron pierced the morning quiet.

Atop one of the tall sand dunes at Springer's Point, Betsy Michaels turned from studying the ocean below and peered behind her at the gnarled oaks of the maritime forest, the last one on Ocracoke Island. A shout from somewhere beyond the forest's edge echoed on the cold wind, and she squinted at the sandy trail leading back through the trees.

She listened for a few seconds and then relaxed. It was only the wind blowing through the trees. She turned back toward the ocean but whirled around again when the crack of two rapid gunshots split the early morning air.

Anger replaced the fear she'd felt moments ago. Guns weren't allowed in the 120-acre protected sanctuary of the North Carolina Coastal Land Trust. She unzipped her fanny pack and pulled out her cell phone. Before she could punch in the number of the Ocracoke sheriff's office, a man stumbled from the thick growth of the forest and reeled toward her.

Blood covered the front of his shirt. He held out a hand toward her. Terrified, Betsy took a step backward. The man hobbled another step before he sank to his knees. "P-please…" he mumbled "…h-help me."

Betsy hesitated a moment, then rushed forward. Horrified, she grabbed his arms and eased him to the ground.

"I'll call the sheriff's office for help." She punched in the first number of the island headquarters where her brother and brother-in-law worked as deputies.

He grimaced with pain and tried to raise his head. "Caught me…"

Betsy's heart pounded at the thought of impending danger. "Is someone following you?"

His hand clutched at her unzipped fanny pack. "Tell him…"

Betsy glanced over her shoulder and scanned the thick trees before she turned back to the man. His hand drifted from her fanny pack to the ground. "Don't talk," she said. "I'll get help for you."

Her sister-in-law, Lisa Michaels, answered on the first ring. "Sheriff's office."

"Lisa, it's Betsy. I'm at Springer's Point with a man who's been shot. He needs help right away."

"I'm notifying EMTs and deputies right now. Stay on the phone with me until they get there. Is it a bad wound?"

"I think so, but…"

The man tugged at her arm. "Decoys," he whispered.

Betsy frowned and glanced across the inlet. Duck hunting season was months away. There were no decoys in sight today. She shook her head. "Hush. Save your strength."

He gritted his teeth and grasped her arm. "Tell him…decoys…not what they seem."

"Tell who?" Her heart lurched at the life fading from his eyes. She bent closer. "Can you hear me?" His chest heaved one last breath, and his body stilled. She nudged his shoulder. "Don't give up. Help will be here soon." When he didn't answer, she pressed her fingers to his wrist but felt no pulse. She clasped his hand in hers and closed her eyes. "Oh, God, please don't let this man die. Give him the strength to hold on until help arrives."

"Betsy? What's going on?" Lisa's voice startled her and her eyes flew open.

Her hand shook as she raised the phone to her ear. "I think he's dead." The thought sent a wave of panic flooding through her. Whoever shot him could be watching her this very moment. She cast a frightened look over her shoulder. "Where are those EMTs?"

"They're in the parking area. They're heading down the trail now, but it's quite a hike to the Point. Are you doing okay?"

Another cold wind blew in from the ocean and Betsy shivered. "I am, but I wish they'd hurry."

"Hey!" a voice yelled. "What are you doing?"

Betsy jumped to her feet and spun to see who had called out. A man stood at the edge of the forest. She gripped her cell phone tighter. "Lisa, a man just came out of the forest."

"Who is he?"

Betsy squinted in an effort to make out his features. At this distance, she could only determine he was tall. "I don't know, but he looks threatening. Are Brock and Scott behind the EMTs?"

"They're both on duty today and are on their way. What's the man doing now?"

Before Betsy could speak, the man charged in her direction. "He's coming toward me."

"Get out of there, Betsy. Now!"

Two options flashed into Betsy's head. Make a run on the trail through the forest or slide down the steep dunes to the small inlet beach below. But she'd never make it through the tangle of flowering yucca and sea oxeye that covered the dunes.

"There's nowhere to go!"

"Does he have a gun?"

"I don't see one." The tactics she'd learned in her self-defense class rushed through her head. Taking a deep breath, Betsy planted her feet in a wide stance and held up her hand. "Stop where you are," she yelled. "I'm on the phone with the police. They'll be here any minute."

The man stopped, then inched forward. He shook his head in disbelief. "Betsy?"

Shivers ran up her spine at the sound of the voice from the past. "Mark?" she gasped. "Mark Webber? Is it really you?"

Moments ago, Betsy had thought her heart would burst with fear, but it was nothing compared to the way it raced at the sight of the man she'd tried to erase from her memory. Her first thought was of how glad she was to see him, but that changed in an instant to suspicion. She glanced behind her in hopes the EMTs were close.

"W-what are you doing on Ocracoke?"

He frowned. "I'll tell you later. You said you called the police." He glanced at the man at her feet. "How is he?"

"I think he's dead."

He rubbed his hand across his head as she remembered seeing him do in the past. Then his dark hair had been thick, but now it was close-cropped and spiked. His former clean-shaven look was gone, and in its place he sported a beard consisting of a thin line of hair extended from his sideburns and along his jawline into a pencil mustache. But the biggest surprise was the spiked leather cuff bracelet he wore and the silver stud in one ear.

He knelt beside the man and checked his pulse before he pushed to his feet. "You're right. He's dead. We'd better wait for the police and let them sort this whole thing out."

Betsy's eyes grew wide at the lack of emotion in Mark's words. What was the matter with him? A man lay dead at their feet, and he acted like it was just a normal day. She glanced down at the dead man again and clenched her fists at her side. Her heart constricted at the thought that somewhere this man had family who had no idea what had happened. Maybe Mark didn't care that a man had lost his life, but she did. But then she'd learned long ago that Mark didn't care for anyone but himself.

Betsy wanted to scream at him, to demand he tell her what had brought him to Springer's Point this morning and why he looked like a rap star who had just stepped offstage. Before she could confront him, he turned his back, walked to the edge of dunes, and stared at the water below. She glanced down at the cell phone in her hand and brought it back to her ear.

"Lisa, are you still there?"

"Betsy, I've been going out of my mind. What's happening there?"

She wished she could answer that question, but at the moment she had no idea. "All I know is there is a dead man on the dunes and a man I used to know came out of the woods. Where are Brock and Scott now?"

"They're right behind the EMTs. They should arrive any minute."

"Thanks, Lisa. I'll talk to you later." She disconnected the call, slipped the cell phone in her fanny pack, and zipped it closed. She felt better knowing Brock, her sister's husband, and her brother were the deputies on duty this morning. Maybe they could get to the bottom of who was responsible for the man's death. Betsy stared at Mark's back, and the need for answers welled up in her. She clenched her fists. "Mark, answer my question. What are you doing on Ocracoke?"

He turned slowly and faced her. "I'm on vacation."

"*Vacation?* You've never come here before." She let her gaze drift over him, and the truth hit her. A bitter taste poured into her mouth and her lip curled into a sneer. "You're undercover again, aren't you?"

His shoulders drooped, and he took a step toward her. "Betsy, I..."

Before he could finish, the EMTs burst from the forest and onto the dunes. She and Mark backed away as they began to work on the man at their feet. Within minutes, Brock and Scott emerged from the trail and rushed toward her.

Scott grabbed her by the arms. "Are you all right?"

She nodded. "I am. Just still a little shaken, though." She glanced at Mark over her shoulder and made the proper introductions.

Scott released her and cleared his throat. "Glad to meet you, Mr. Webber. What were you doing at Springer's Point this morning?"

"Out sightseeing." Surprise flickered in Mark's eyes, and he glanced at Betsy. "I didn't know you had a brother. I thought you just had two sisters."

Brock turned a puzzled look toward her. "Betsy, do you know this man?" Brock asked.

"Yes, but I haven't seen him in years." She glanced at Mark. "As for my brother, his mother was our father's first wife. We were reunited a few years ago."

His eyes darted from Scott to Brock. "I see."

The muscle in Scott's jaw twitched, but he didn't speak. After a few seconds he pulled a notepad from his pocket. "Betsy, can you tell us what happened?"

He wrote as she related the events of the morning. When she'd finished, he flipped the notepad closed. "Brock, do you have any questions for Betsy?"

Brock, who'd been unusually quiet since he appeared on the scene, shook his head. "I think we need to find out where the shooting occurred. Since Betsy told us where he emerged from the forest, we need to get busy." He turned to Mark. "Maybe you heard something while you were sightseeing, like what direction the shots came from."

Mark nodded. "I don't know much, but I'll be glad to help any way I can."

Brock gritted his teeth and took a step closer to the body. He bent forward and stared down at the still figure. Arnold Culver, one of the EMTs, rose to his feet. "There's nothing we can do for this guy, Brock. There's no identification on the body. In fact there's nothing in his pockets at all. Even the label has been cut out of his shirt. That seems strange."

Brock and Scott exchanged quick glances. "We'll start checking around the island. Maybe somebody knows him," Brock said.

Arnold nodded. "It would be a shame if he has family waiting in some motel." The EMT rubbed his chin and cocked an eyebrow. "But if he does, it looks like he'd have some kind of identification. At least a driver's license."

"Yeah, it sure does."

Arnold shrugged. "Is it okay if we transport him to the health center?"

Brock stared at the body a moment before he exhaled. "Yeah, go ahead. We'll stay and look for the murder scene. I'll stop by the health center when we get back to the village." He glanced over his shoulder at Betsy. "I saw your bicycle in the parking lot. I'd rather you didn't ride it back to the village. After all, there's a murderer somewhere out here. Go back with Arnold and I'll bring your bike to the station. Okay?"

She was tempted to ask Mark if he would be going to the station, too. When she glanced at him, a veil descended over his eyes, and she knew she'd been right when she asked if he was under-cover again. She had seen that look before. Betsy pulled her attention away from Mark and waited until Arnold and his assistant had finished bag-ging the body.

Arnold smiled at her. "Ready to go, Betsy?"

"Yes." She glanced one more time at Mark, but he still hadn't looked at her.

Brock hooked his thumbs in his service belt and inclined his head toward the forest. "Okay, Mr. Webber, suppose you show us where you were when you heard the shots."

Without speaking, Mark headed toward the spot where he'd exited the forest. Brock and Scott followed behind. She stared at Mark's back a moment, and the memory of his walking away from her once before washed over her. With one last glance in his direction, she jogged after Arnold and his assistant, who had already disappeared down the trail.

As she hurried to catch up with the EMTs, she thought about the look in Mark's eyes when he'd first seen her. Was it surprise, or was it something else? Could he possibly have been happy to see her? She frowned and shook her head. Thinking like that could get her in trouble. It had once before.

Whatever he felt when he first saw her, it had changed in an instant. The old Mark had emerged and brought back all the memories she'd tried to push from her mind. The veiled look had alerted her to what she wished she'd seen when she first met him.

How she wished she could forget what had happened, but she couldn't. Even after all these years she still remembered the terror she felt the night two officers escorted her into a police department interrogation room. That fear had turned to anger when Mark walked into the room and advised her it would go easier on her if she told the police everything she knew. Then he walked out the door and left her to face the worst nightmare of her life.

She'd called out for him to come back that night, but he walked away without a backward glance. Just like he did moments ago when he went with Brock and Scott. Now she only wanted to get away from him as fast as she could.

Mark was on the hunt, just like before, and he'd once again gone into shutdown mode. She had no idea who he was after, but she knew one thing. He didn't care who he had to walk all over in the pursuit of justice.

This time, she was determined it wouldn't be her.

Mark braced himself for the outburst he knew was coming. They had barely entered the forest before it happened.

"That's far enough, Webber." Brock's voice brought him to a halt. "What in the world were you thinking?"

He took a deep breath and stared at the deputies. The branches of a huge tree shaded the three of them, but it didn't hide the anger on their faces. Both of them glared at him with looks that told him they'd like to punch him in the jaw.

"I had no idea you were related to Betsy."

"Are you serious?" Scott hissed. "The Drug Enforcement Administration gives you an undercover assignment on the island where Betsy grew up, and you don't think it's important they know about your connection?"

He shook his head. "I knew she was from Ocracoke, but I didn't know for sure she came back here after she graduated from art school. She told me she wanted to live in New York." He glanced at Brock. "When I met with you at Sheriff Baxter's office on the mainland, I had no clue you were related to Betsy. And you, Scott, weren't even there. If you had been, I probably wouldn't have made the connection. I didn't even know Betsy had a brother."

Scott took a step closer to Mark. "I know all about Betsy's experience with an undercover police officer in Memphis. If we had known it was you, we would have told Sheriff Baxter to send you back to Raleigh."

"Well, I'm here now, and you'll have to make the best of it," Mark countered.

Scott clenched his fists. "I'm warning you, Webber. Watch your step around my sister. Understand?"

Brock laid a restraining hand on Scott's arm. "I suppose there's no use arguing about it now. We've got bigger problems. The murdered guy back there is John Draper. He's been working undercover for several months here. He must have found out something that got him killed. Do you have any idea what it could be?"

Mark shook his head. "All I know is I was assigned to take over the investigation here. Draper was supposed to leave on the noon ferry today. I received instructions to rendezvous with him at Springer's Point this morning. He had something to give me. When I arrived, he was dead."

Brock pulled off his sunglasses and stuck them in his shirt pocket. "Do you have any idea what he had for you?"

"No. My message just said he'd made a big discovery that could blow the case open, and I was to meet him here. But according to the EMTs he didn't have anything in his pockets."

Brock's forehead wrinkled. "Do you think he could have hidden it somewhere?"

Mark shrugged. "I don't know." His heart pounded at a sudden thought. "I wonder if he could have said anything to Betsy. Maybe something that didn't seem important at the time."

"That's a possibility. We'll see if she remembers anything." Brock sighed and stared into the forest. "Before we do, let's see if we can find the spot where he was shot. Could you tell where the sound came from?"

Mark pointed deeper into the forest. "This way. I was on the trail when I heard the gunfire and ran into the trees. I didn't see anyone until I found Betsy bending over him."

"Then let's try straight ahead," Brock said.

A sudden thought popped into Mark's head, and his eyes grew wide. "Wait a minute. Whoever shot John must have followed him when he stumbled out of the forest. What if they saw Betsy? She could be in danger. We need to question her to see if there's something she saw that may be related to John's death."

Scott's mouth tightened. "I don't want my sister to be dragged into the middle of an undercover drug sting."

"And neither do I," Brock added.

"I understand." It was evident the two deputies were very protective of her, and Mark didn't blame them.

His friendship with Betsy had died years ago, and there was no point in thinking it could be recovered. He'd tried over and over to explain what had happened, but she wouldn't answer his phone calls or emails. Then when he'd worked up his courage, he'd finally gone to her apartment to beg her forgiveness. That gesture had earned him a door slammed in his face.

Only then did he give up. Betsy hated him and would never forgive him. He'd accepted what he couldn't change. Or had he? Maybe when he'd received this assignment, he'd secretly hoped she might be on Ocracoke.

He gritted his teeth and shook his head. Forget that idea and concentrate on the job. A DEA agent had been murdered, and Betsy had been the last person to see him alive. She might have information that would be helpful in catching a killer. That's all he wanted from her. Nothing more.

He had two goals—catch John's killer and bring down a drug-smuggling ring. When that was accomplished, he'd be off this island and out of Betsy Michaels's life for good.

TWO

Betsy stopped pacing the floor of the small office in the Ocracoke Sheriff's Department and glanced at her watch. "What's keeping them? They should have been here an hour ago."

Lisa, the department dispatcher and Scott's recent bride, looked up from her computer screen and smiled. "They'll be here as soon as they're finished at Springer's Point. When Scott called in, he said they thought they'd found the spot where the man was shot. They're looking for any evidence left at the scene."

Betsy sank down in a chair by her sister-in-law's desk and covered her face with her hands. "Oh, Lisa, it was awful. That poor man. He died right beside me and I don't know who he is or where he's from."

"I'm sure Brock and Scott will be able to tell us more when they get here." Lisa reached out and patted Betsy's shoulder before she directed her gaze back to the computer.

Betsy twisted in her chair and propped her elbows on Lisa's desk. "Did Scott say anything about Mark Webber when he called in?"

A frown creased Lisa's forehead, but she didn't pull her attention from her computer. "Like what?"

"Like whether or not he's coming back to the station with them?"

"No, but with him being a witness, too, they'll probably bring him back."

Betsy slumped in her chair and crossed her arms. "That's what I thought."

Lisa stopped typing, her fingers hovering over the computer keyboard, and stared at Betsy. "You sound like you don't want to see him."

Betsy's face grew warm, and she blew at a stray lock of hair that dangled on her forehead. "I thought I'd seen him for the last time, and then he shows up again."

Lisa tilted her head to the side and frowned. "I don't understand. Had you met him before today?"

Betsy grunted and scooted down farther in her chair. "Oh, yeah."

"But when? I've never heard you talk about anyone named Mark Webber."

Betsy sighed and straightened. "I met Mark when I was in art school in Memphis. I worked part-time as a hostess at a restaurant, and Mark was a waiter there."

"Oh, yeah. I remember Kate talking about your job. She showed me some pictures she took of the restaurant when she visited you once."

"It was a great place to work, and the job was just what I needed, especially after I got that letter from Kevin saying he'd changed his mind about marrying me. He'd fallen in love with Sherry Kincaid, the girl who hated me all through school."

Lisa pushed her computer keyboard out of the way and crossed her arms on top of the desk. "Yeah, he was a jerk. But I always thought he wasn't good enough for you. He might have been the star athlete when we were in school, but look at him now. He can't keep a steady job, and he and Sherry have three kids to feed. I'll bet she'd change places with you in a heartbeat."

Betsy reached over and squeezed her sister-in-law's hand. "I doubt it, but you're sweet to say that. Anyway, it's all in the past. Back then, I was hurt and felt betrayed. Mark Webber was handsome and always seemed to have a lot of money to spend. But I couldn't understand why he asked me questions all the time about our boss. Mr.Rousseau, the owner, had been good to me and helped me through the rough spot with Kevin. I decided Mark must think we were involved. I liked Mr. Rousseau a lot, but that's as far as the relationship went."

"So what happened next?"

"Mark really seemed to want a friendship with me, and soon I began to think he liked me. You know, in a more personal way. He kept asking me out, and when I finally gave in, I found I really liked him. In fact, I thought we might be headed for something serious. That is, until I learned the truth."

Lisa's eyes grew wide. "What truth?"

"Mr. Rousseau was the head of a drug ring, and the restaurant was a front for the organization. The police raided the place one night, and I discovered Mark was an undercover police officer who thought I was involved in the drug ring." She swallowed hard. "So all the time he pretended to be interested in me, he really wanted to get some evidence against my boss and arrest me as an accomplice."

"Oh, Betsy," Lisa whispered, "how awful."

"Yeah, it was. The officers took me downtown to police headquarters to question me. I was so relieved when Mark walked into the interrogation room, until I realized he thought I was guilty."

Betsy wiped at the tears forming in her eyes. Even now it hurt to talk about that night.

Lisa wrapped her fingers around Betsy's hand. "I can't believe anyone who knows you could suspect you'd be involved in something like that."

"I begged Mark to believe me, but he walked out and left me there. Later, I think he was really disappointed when he found out I had nothing to do with the drugs."

Lisa's fingers tightened. "What a jerk. I hope he does come in here. I'd like to give him a piece of my mind."

Betsy took a deep breath and shook her head. "It wouldn't do any good. I'm sure he thought he was doing his job and didn't care who got hurt in the process. I'll have to give him credit for trying to apologize later, but it came too late. He lied to me—just like Kevin did when he said he'd be here waiting until I finished school. Bottom line…I knew I could never trust him."

"And now he shows up here. I wonder why."

Betsy snickered. "I don't have to guess. I know from the way he looked, he's undercover again. The problem is, I don't know who he's after. But whoever it is, Mark had better stay away from me."

Before Lisa could respond, the front door opened, and Scott and Brock walked in with Mark right behind. Lisa shot a glaring look at Mark as Scott walked over and put his arm around Betsy's shoulder. "How are you doing?"

She pushed her hair behind her ear and straightened her shoulders. "I'm fine. Lisa's been keeping me company. I thought you'd never get here…"

"It took us longer out at Springer's Point than we'd thought," Brock said. He pointed to the back of the room. "Let's go in my office and talk about what happened this morning."

Without glancing in Mark's direction, Betsy followed Brock and Scott into the office. Mark's footsteps behind sent a warning signal flaring through her. When they entered Brock's office and the door closed, she could sense Mark's presence. She jerked her head in his direction. "What's he doing here?"

Brock and Scott looked straight at her. "We thought we'd talk to the two witnesses together," Brock said.

Betsy crossed her arms and sighed. "Don't try to be evasive with me, Brock. I suspect Mark is an undercover officer." She turned to face Mark. "I also know the Memphis Police Department has no jurisdiction on Ocracoke. So who do you work for now?"

"Betsy, please don't…" Brock began.

She held out her hand with her palm facing Brock and shook her head. "No. I will not be tricked again by this man." She turned to Mark. "Are you here to investigate me? Do you still think I must be involved in something illegal?"

Mark's Adam's apple bobbed. "Betsy, I never expected to see you when I came here. It was as much a surprise to me as it was to you."

She took a step toward him. "Then be honest with me for a change. Why are you here?"

Neither of them blinked as they stared into each other's eyes. Brock was the one to finally break the silence. "Mark, Betsy's whole family has been involved in law enforcement as long as she can remember. She knows how important it is to keep matters confidential. You're going to have to trust her."

Mark's forehead crinkled. "I do trust her, even if she doesn't believe me." He took a deep breath. "Betsy, I'm with the Drug Enforcement Administration stationed in Raleigh now. I'm undercover on Ocracoke to bring down a drug ring that's smuggling illegal drugs into the country. The man murdered today was John Draper. He's been undercover here for the past few months. I came to the island to replace him. Now it looks like I'll be helping find his killer, and I think you can help."

Betsy blinked in surprise. "How?"

"I received a message from him that he had some information for me and wanted to show me some evidence he'd discovered. But there was nothing on his body. Did he give you anything?"

"Like what?"

Mark shrugged. "I have no idea. All I know is he had something he said would blow our case wide open. I thought maybe he gave it to you."

She shook her head. "No. He didn't have time to give me anything. He died right away."

Mark inched closer. "He must have done something with whatever it was. Think, Betsy. What happened after he came out of the forest?"

The events of the morning replayed in her mind, and she frowned in thought. "When I got to him, he said something about being caught. I thought he meant in the forest, but I didn't see anybody else. Then I told him I was calling the sheriff's office, and he mumbled something that sounded like 'tell him.'"

"Tell him what?" Brock asked.

She shook her head. "I don't know. I told him to be still, and he said something about decoys. I thought he was delirious and maybe was thinking about duck season."

Mark rubbed his hand over his head. "Did he just say the word decoy?"

"No. He said the decoys weren't what they seemed. Then he gasped for breath, and I thought he had died. I closed my eyes and prayed for him, but it was no use. He was dead."

Scott touched her arm, and she turned to him. "Are you sure he didn't do or say anything else?"

She shook her head again. "No, that's all he said." She glanced from Scott to Brock. "If there was anything else, I would tell you. But that's all he said."

Brock let out a long breath. "We just want to make sure. If you think of anything else, let us know right away."

"I will. Now is it okay if I go? I'm supposed to do some volunteer work at the British Cemetery today. I need to run by Treasury's bed-and-breakfast and check on Emma before I go over there."

"Who's Emma?" Mark asked.

"My little sister," Betsy said. "She lives with me in our family home out close to the beach. Scott lived with us until he and Lisa married recently."

Mark nodded. "I do remember you telling me about her. How old is she now?"

"Eleven."

Scott smiled. "Tell my little sister I'll see her later."

"I will." She turned to leave, but Mark stepped in front of her and blocked her way.

His dark eyes stared at her. "Be careful. There's still a killer out there somewhere."

She lifted her chin and returned the intense gaze. "There may be a murderer on the island, but it has nothing to do with me. I'm not involved, just like I wasn't the last time."

He clenched his jaw and stepped out of her way. Betsy nodded to Scott and Brock and strode from the office. Lisa was on the phone and didn't look up as Betsy rushedby. It was just as well, Betsy thought. She needed to get out of the office. Being around Mark brought up too many memories, and she didn't need to dwell on things that happened years ago.

When she stepped onto the sidewalk, she saw her bicycle leaning against the side of the building. She jumped on and pedaled down the street toward Treasury Wilkes's bed-and-breakfast. Whenever she needed someone to talk to, she ran to Treasury, who had been like a second mother ever since her own mother had died when Betsy was sixteen.

When she reached the two-story Victorian, she rushed inside, but Treasury and Emma were nowhere to be seen. They were probably off on one of their morning walks on the beach and wouldn't be back until the middle of the afternoon.

Betsy glanced at her watch and was surprised to see that it was only ten o'clock. She had time to do her work at the cemetery before lunch. She hurried out the back door of the house to her truck, which she'd parked here this morning before her trip to Springer's Point. Her gardening tools lay in the truck bed.

She grabbed the keys from under the driver's seat and within minutes was on her way to the small cemetery where she spent time each week. The only way she knew to rid her mind of the events of the morning was to work off her pent-up energy on one of her projects. The British Cemetery topped the list of her favorite island spots.

She wanted to forget everything about the morning at Springer's Point, especially the part about seeing Mark again. When she left Memphis, she thought Mark Webber was out of her life for good. Now he'd shown up undercover on her island. She couldn't afford to let him into her life again, especially since she'd once thought they could have something special together.

Maybe a few hours of hard work and perspiration would erase that silly notion from her head.

Mark found it difficult to keep his mind on what Brock and Scott were saying. His mind kept wandering to the events earlier today. His gaze flitted across Brock's office and came to a stop on a photograph sitting on a bookshelf behind Brock's desk. Two women and a young girl smiled at him from the frame. One of them was Betsy.

Brock glanced at him and noticed him staring at the picture. "That's my wife, Kate, and her two sisters. Emma is the youngest one's name, and of course you know Betsy."

He nodded. "Yeah. You can tell they're sisters. They look alike."

Brock picked up a paper off his desk and continued his discussion on leads John Draper had passed on to their office since his arrival on the island, but Mark tuned him out as he stared at Betsy's picture. All he'd thought about all morning was how beautiful she looked at Springer's Point. She'd almost looked happy to see him in that first moment, but it passed quickly. A scowl replaced the smile, and he realized he was dreaming if he thought she'd ever welcome the sight of him again. Still, he couldn't erase the picture of her standing at the top of the dunes—her feet planted apart, her dark eyes flashing, and her chestnut colored hair blowing in the breeze.

It reminded him of the night he began working in the Memphis restaurant and how he thought he'd never seen a more beautiful girl than Betsy, who was working as hostess. Although he kept telling himself to be careful about becoming too friendly with her, he couldn't help liking her. In the end, though, he'd made a mess of that friendship like he had every other one he'd ever tried to have.

He sighed and directed his attention back to Brock Gentry. "What did you say?"

Brock chuckled. "What are you thinking about? You seem distracted."

Mark pushed to his feet and shook his head. "I can't get Draper out of my mind, and I'm tired. I didn't sleep much last night. I think I need a cup of coffee."

Scott jumped to his feet. "We can take care of that. Lisa keeps the coffee pot ready. Come on to the break room with me. You want some, Brock?"

Brock shook his head. "No, you two go on. I need to work on this report about Draper's death."

Mark followed Scott into the outer office. The woman who'd been at the dispatcher's desk entered from a back room with a cup of coffee in her hand. She stopped as Scott approached her, and her eyes sparkled with a message meant for him alone. Scott smiled and leaned toward her.

"Me, too," he whispered. Then he cleared his throat and straightened. "Uh, Mark, this is my wife, Lisa. We're still newlyweds. I can't believe this gorgeous woman would marry a guy like me."

Mark smiled. "Congratulations. It's nice to meet you, Mrs. Michaels. I'm Mark Webber."

The smile on her face disappeared, and her eyes narrowed. "I've heard a lot about you, Mr. Webber. From Betsy. She's not only my sister-in-law, she's a good friend. And I might add, she's a wonderful woman."

"I couldn't agree with you more."

Scott raised his hand to his mouth to cover a slight cough. "I told Mark I'd get him a cup of coffee. Is there any left?"

Lisa Michaels pursed her lips, nodded, and walked back to her desk. Mark took a step to follow Scott into the break room but stopped when the front door opened. A man in cutoff jeans, a T-shirt and a floppy straw hat strolled into the room and sauntered over to where Mark and Scott stood.

The man pushed his long gray hair behind his ear and grinned at Scott. "I heard there was some trouble out to the Point this morning. You got any idea who shot that feller?"

Scott sighed. "Mark, meet Grady Teach. He's always the first to know whatever happens on the island, and he likes to spread the word. Grady, this is Mark Webber. He's vacationing on the island."

"Glad to meet you." Grady grinned, and his tongue poked through a gap in the bottom row of his teeth. "Now about that feller that got shot. I happened to be at the health center when Arnold brought the body in, and I heard Doc talking 'bout how they didn't know who he was. So I offered to look and see if I knew him."

Scott arched an eyebrow. "Now, Grady. Don't tell me Doc let you look at the body?"

Grady waved a hand in dismissal. "Well, he may not have known I looked, but I told him afterward I'd seen that feller over at the Blue Pelican a few nights ago. He was a-sittin' at the bar like he was waitin' for somebody."

"Had you ever seen him there before?" Scott asked.

"No, but it seems like I saw him somewhere else. If I think of it, I'll let you know. You got any idea who he is?"

Scott shook his head, put his hand on Grady's shoulder and ushered him to the door. "I've got nothing to tell you, Grady, but thanks for stopping by and let me know if you think of anything else."

When the door closed behind Grady, Scott turned around. "I'll tell Brock we need to check out the Blue Pelican and see if anybody knows who Draper met there. Grady always knows just enough to try and find out more. He's faster than a text message when it comes to spreading gossip. Now how about that coffee?"

Mark shook his head. "I think I'll pass. Maybe I'll get some later. I need to talk to my superiors and see where we go from here."

Scott nodded. "See you later."

Mark nodded to Lisa, who glanced up as he strode toward the door, exited the police station and hurried to his car. Once inside he pulled out his cell phone and dialed the DEA office in Raleigh. Moments later he was connected with his superior and related the account of John Draper's death.

"What about this girl who was with him?" the special agent in charge asked.

Mark hesitated before he answered. "She's a local artist. She says he didn't give her anything, and I've told you what she said were his last words."

"I don't know, Mark. There may be something she's forgotten. I think you need to question her again."

"I don't think that's necessary. I believed her."

"Nevertheless, I'm telling you to talk to her.

Don't give up until you know for sure. Understand?" The voice vibrated with authority, and Mark knew it would no good to argue.

He sighed. "Okay, whatever you say. I'll keep you posted."

Mark ended the call and started the engine. Where was it Betsy said she was going? Some cemetery, but where?

He pulled into the street and spotted Grady Teach standing on the sidewalk outside the Coffee Cup. Mark pulled to the curb and rolled down his window. "Hey, Grady. I met you over at the sheriff's office a few minutes ago, and I wondered if you can help me."

Grady sauntered over to the car and leaned against the door. "What with?"

"A friend of mine was going to some special cemetery this morning, but I've forgotten the name."

"Oh, that's easy. All the tourists want to see the British Cemetery. Take Highway 12 until you come to British Cemetery Road and turn left. Can't miss it."

"Thanks, Grady." Mark waved and rolled the window up.

Taking a deep breath, Mark eased down on the accelerator. His boss was right. He needed to question Betsy more and see if there was something she'd forgotten. He didn't want to intrude into her life, but a DEA agent had been killed. She might know something that would help them find the killer. Another thought struck him. She also might know something that would put her in danger. If so, he needed to find the killer as quickly as possible.

His fingers tightened on the cell phone when the name flashed on the caller ID. He pressed the phone to his ear. "Do you have it?"

"No. There was a problem."

He sank down in his desk chair and wiped at the perspiration that popped out on his forehead. "What do you mean there was a problem?"

"Draper is dead, but he got out of the forest before we could reach him. We followed his trail out to the Point, but there was a woman with him. I had her in my sights and was about to shoot when this guy ran out of the forest. We heard her say the police were on their way. We couldn't risk sticking around."

He jumped to his feet, and the chair tipped backward and landed on the floor. "But you could risk the police finding what Draper had?"

The sigh that answered his question chilled his blood. "What Draper had is your problem. We were only trying to help you out. Our friends sent us here to make sure this next shipment gets to the mainland. After that, you're the one who's going to have to answer to why you couldn't stop a DEA agent when you found him rifling through your office files."

His heart slammed against his chest. "You don't have to remind me. I need to recover whatever Draper found out. I'll make it well worth your while if you can get it for me."

Silence greeted his offer. He waited and finally his caller spoke. "We'll see what we can do. We have information that there was nothing on his body when he was brought in. We also know the woman at the Point is an artist named Betsy Michaels. We think Draper probably gave the item to her, and the police may already have it. Want us to put some pressure on her to tell us where it is?"

A smile pulled at his lips, and he reached down and set the chair upright. "Yes, but be careful. Everybody in her family works for the sheriff's department."

"In that case, this could be trickier. It's going to cost you twice what we usually get paid."

"No problem. Just get it back for me before that shipment leaves."

"We'll see what we can do."

He disconnected the call and tossed the cell phone on his desk. "Betsy," he muttered, "why did you have to get mixed up in this? It would have been better if you had stayed home this morning."

He sat at his desk for a few moments thinking about John Draper and wishing he had killed him when he'd caught him snooping. Instead the man's escape had put the entire drug cartel in jeopardy. When the bosses on the mainland looked for the weak link in their organization, he knew they would look to him for answers. He had to do whatever was necessary to protect himself, even sending those hired assassins after Betsy Michaels.

That decision should bother him, but it didn't. He had too much riding on this last shipment to worry about Betsy. The Michaels family had a reputation as protectors of the island and its residents. Too bad they wouldn't be able to do anything to help their sister. She had just come on the radar of the wrong people, and they never stopped until they got what they wanted.

THREE

After an hour of weeding the British Cemetery, Betsy began to feel more relaxed. Her time spent in the small plot the island residents held in high esteem always made her misty-eyed and thankful for patriotic men like those buried here. They'd given the ultimate sacrifice in the pursuit of freedom. Her brother, Scott, had almost met the same fate, and she thanked God every day for his life.

Kneeling beside the sign that identified the small cemetery as a piece of English soil, she patted the last pansy into the flower bed and sat back on her heels to admire her handiwork. She glanced over her shoulder at the four graves and scanned them in search of an elusive weed she had missed.

"That's a beautiful flower bed." The lilting drawl drifted from the edge of the street.

Betsy glanced up and into the face of two smiling women. The brims of straw hats shaded their faces, but wisps of gray hair stuck out over their ears. Sunglasses perched on their noses, and they each held one of the information pamphlets from the Island Visitors Center.

Betsy pushed to her feet and brushed the dirt from the gardening gloves she wore. "Thank you. May I help you?"

One of them pointed to the pamphlet she held. "We're vacationing on the island and wanted to get a look at the British Cemetery. We didn't expect to find someone working here."

Betsy walked to where they stood and smiled. "The Coast Guard is in charge of keeping the grounds in order. I know the guys stationed on the island, so I volunteer to help them out every once in a while. My name is Betsy Michaels."

The woman who had spoken pointed to the woman beside her. "This is my friend Miranda Walton, and I'm Lizzy Nichols. We're retired teachers from Florida, and we're vacationing on your beautiful island."

"I hope you're enjoying your visit."

Miranda nodded. "It's been wonderful, but this is the first time we've gotten over here to see the cemetery. We understand there's quite a story behind it."

"There is." Betsy pointed to the pamphlets they held. "Does it tell about it there?"

Lizzy held hers up and scanned it. "A little, but there must be more."

Miranda inched closer. "Do you know what happened to the men buried here? If you do, I'd love to hear the story."

"I'd like to hear it, too." The familiar voice sent shock waves rippling through Betsy's body, and she looked past Miranda and Lizzy to Mark who stood in the street behind the women.

The visitors glanced at him and turned back to her with big smiles on their faces. "It sounds like you've been chosen to serve as a tour guide for us. Please tell us what happened."

Betsy licked her lips and watched Mark stroll up to stand behind Lizzy. Her heart pounded so she didn't know if she could speak. She took a deep breath and tried to smile. "All right."

Miranda motioned to Mark. "Young man, step up here beside us so you can hear."

He moved closer, and Betsy cleared her throat. "During the early days of World War II, German U-boats attacked merchant ships off the eastern coast of the United States. From January to June of 1942, almost four hundred ships were sunk off our coast. That's when the area first became known as the Graveyard of the Atlantic."

Lizzy nodded. "My class studied about that when we covered World War II."

"England sent a fleet of ships to patrol the shipping lanes, and the HMS *Bedfordshire,* was one of them. On the morning of May 14, 1942, two bodies washed up on Ocracoke, and their papers identified them as crewman on the *Bedfordshire*. Several more bodies as well as wreckage from the torpedoed ship followed. The island residents buried them in a spot they designated as the British Cemetery. They later ceded the land to England for all time."

Miranda stared at the graves. "I was just a baby when my father died in the war. My mother never recovered. It's sad to think of the families whose loved ones didn't come home."

"It is. But each year," Betsy said, "representatives from England and members of our military come together for a ceremony to honor the men who gave their lives in the pursuit of freedom."

Lizzy wiped at a tear in the corner of her eye. "What a touching story, and you tell it so well."

Betsy darted a glance at Mark, and her heart thudded at the intense stare he directed at her.

His Adam's apple bobbed. "Yes, you do."

Lizzy and Miranda stared at him, then looked at each other and smiled. Lizzy patted Miranda's arm. "I think we need to be on our way. Maybe we'll see you again."

Betsy smiled. "I hope so, too. Enjoy your vacation."

Neither she nor Mark spoke until the two women had walked some distance down the street.

Then he sighed. "I suppose you're wondering what I'm doing here."

The tightness in her chest kept her from speaking at first, but she took a deep breath and tried again. "How did you find me?"

He ran his hand through his hair and grinned. "I couldn't remember where you told your brother you'd be, but I knew it was a cemetery. So I asked the one person on the island who seems to know everything, and he told me."

She smiled. "Grady Teach?"

Mark laughed, and she remembered how that sound used to thrill her.

"That's the guy," he said. "It seems this is one of the most visited tourist spots on the island, and now I understand why." He stared at the graves a moment. "Listening to you tell the story of how these men died made me think of my parents."

His words surprised Betsy. "I don't remember you ever talking about your parents."

"I don't talk about them much. They died when I was twelve years old." He took a deep breath. "But I didn't come here to talk about that. I wanted to make sure you're all right."

She narrowed her eyes. "Of course I'm all right. Why would you think I wasn't?"

He glanced around as if he wanted to make sure no one was near enough to hear and then took a step closer. "A man who'd been shot collapsed and died at your feet this morning. Whoever killed him could have seen you. I think you need to be careful." He raised his hand and swept it in a wide arc. "You're out in the open at a tourist attraction in the middle of the day. It could be dangerous."

She pulled the gardening gloves from her hand and tossed them in the basket that held her trowel and pruning shears. "You're being ridiculous."

He glanced up and down the street that ran in front of the cemetery. "This is off the beaten path from the main street of the village. I'm only concerned about your safety."

Betsy propped her hands on her hips. "Yeah, I've heard that before. It seems like that was what you said after Mr. Rousseau's arrest. Your friendship with me was an attempt to keep me safe. Well, I didn't buy it then—and I don't now."

"Betsy, please. What happened this morning has nothing to do with Memphis."

"Maybe not to you, but I can't help remembering how I felt when you thought I was a criminal."

"Betsy…"

Before he could continue, her cell phone chimed. Betsy held up her hand to stop him. She unzipped her fanny pack and pulled it out. Mark's lips twitched when he spotted the phone's hard cover with its painted swirl of butterflies and flowers. "What's wrong?" she said.

He arched an eyebrow. "I've never seen a cover like that."

"I'm an artist. I like bright colors." She dropped her gaze to the phone's screen. The number on the caller ID wasn't familiar. "Hello."

"Where is it?" the raspy voice rattled in her ear.

She pulled the phone away and stared at it for a moment before she raised it back to her ear. "Excuse me. Who is this?"

"A friend."

Betsy frowned and cast a quick glance at Mark. He stepped closer. "Who is it?" he whispered.

She shrugged and spoke again. "You have the wrong number."

"No, I don't."

"I don't like prank calls, mister," Betsy snarled. "Don't call this number again." She punched the end button and slipped her phone back in her fanny pack.

"Who was that?" A worried frown creased Mark's forehead.

"Wrong number." She gave the fanny pack's zipper a quick tug and reached for the basket at her feet. "Now if you'll excuse me, I need to get going. Good luck catching whoever you're after this time."

She brushed past him and headed toward her truck that was parked on the opposite side of the street. Her fingers gripped the basket's handle tighter as she stepped onto the roadway. Her mind whirled with questions. Why had Mark gone out of his way to find her? She doubted if he really had concerns about her safety. He had allowed her to continue working in the dangerous environment of the Memphis restaurant without ever warning her. Of course at the time, he had thought she was involved in the operation.

Ever since she'd first seen him this morning, her head had been spinning with all kinds of thoughts she didn't want to remember. All she wanted was to get away from him as quickly as possible. Working on her latest painting would help her push these troubling thoughts from her head.

A car engine's roar shattered the quiet, and Betsy stared down the street to her left. Her chest constricted at the sight of a black car speeding toward her. Her mind screamed for her to get out of its path, but her feet wouldn't move.

Her body seemed to have switched off its power, and she had the feeling she'd stepped into a movie's slow-motion scene. She willed her legs to move, but they didn't respond.

"Betsy, look out!" Mark's cry came from behind her.

The car roared closer, only a few feet from her at the edge of the cemetery. She closed her eyes just as a heavy weight slammed into her from behind and pushed her forward. The basket flew out of her hand and bounced off the hood of the car as Mark's arms encircled her and propelled her forward. They both skidded to a stop facedown on the pavement beside her truck.

In an instant, Mark was on his feet and staring at the car that disappeared in the distance. Then he dropped back to the ground beside her and helped her sit up. "Are you all right? The car was too far away to get a license plate number."

Betsy winced at the pain in her knees. Her eyes grew wide at the blood trailing down her legs where the skin had been scraped away. She wanted to clamp her hands over the wounds, but her palms burned as if they were on fire. She flexed her fingers. "Next time, I'll wear jeans instead of shorts."

Mark bent over her and examined the cuts. "This doesn't look as bad as it could have been. Are you sure you're all right?"

"I'm fine, just a little banged up."

As she started to get up, he grasped her arm and helped her to her feet. "I think we need to go to the health center and get you checked out."

She shook her head. "No, I'll be fine."

He pulled out his cell phone. "We can do this one of two ways. I'll take you to the health center, or I'll call your brother and tell him you were almost hit by a car. Which will it be?"

She sighed and nodded. "Okay. Do you want to follow me in your car?"

"You don't think I'm going to let you drive after what just happened, do you? You're riding with me. We can get your truck later."

Betsy opened her mouth to argue, but she could tell by the look on his face that it would do no good. "Okay, have it your way. But would you mind getting my gardening tools out of the street before we leave?"

"Sure. Go on and get in my car. It's parked at the edge of the cemetery."

Betsy watched Mark begin to pick up the scattered tools from the street before she turned and hobbled toward his vehicle. The near-miss with the car had left her with more than a few scrapes and scratches. Her skin prickled in fear at the thought that she'd almost been run over.

She'd never felt that scared before, and she hoped she never would again. Her inability to respond to the immediate danger baffled her. Why hadn't she jumped out of the way instead of standing in the street like a frightened animal, not knowing which way to turn? If it hadn't been for Mark, she might be dead now.

She stopped at the door of his car and stared back at him. No matter what she thought about Mark on a personal level, she had to admit his law enforcement training had served him well.

He had reacted like a trained professional, and she owed him a debt of gratitude. Maybe her gratitude would help her overcome the hurt he'd inflicted on her in the past. Then again, maybe nothing could change how she felt. Only time would tell.

Thirty minutes later, Mark flipped a magazine closed and tossed it onto the table at the end of the couch in the health center waiting room. He glanced at his watch and yawned before he pushed to his feet. What could be taking the doctor so long with Betsy?

The front door burst open, and Scott Michaels and Brock Gentry rushed in. They hurried over to him. "Where is she?" Scott demanded.

"Dr. Hunter has her in the examining room. He told me to wait out here until he gets her checked out."

Brock glanced at the closed door leading to the hallway that housed the exam rooms. "What happened?"

Before Mark could answer, the front door burst open again, and a woman Mark had never seen ran into the room. A mesh baby carrier strapped to her body held a baby whose head rested against her chest. She hurried toward Brock, and he put his arm around her.

"How is she?"

"Doc Hunter's with her now." He turned to

Mark. "Mark, this is my wife, Kate. She's Betsy's sister. Kate, this is Mark Webber."

A frown flitted across her face. "Mark Webber from Memphis?"

The icy tone of her voice made his skin tingle. Was he going to get the cold shoulder every time he met a member of Betsy's family? But he supposed he deserved whatever they thought of him. "I used to live in Memphis. I don't anymore." He glanced at the sleeping baby. "That's a cute baby you've got there, Brock."

Brock's eyes softened as he gazed down at his sleeping son, and he brushed a hand across the baby's head. "Yeah, we're proud of him."

Kate turned a pleading look to her husband. "I want to know what happened to Betsy."

"Mark was just about to tell us."

Mark cleared his throat and related how a car had almost hit Betsy at the cemetery. He left out his mounting suspicions about the incident because he wanted to question Betsy about it first.

He had just finished telling them about the near miss when the hallway door opened, and the doctor stepped out. Betsy's family surrounded him before he could move farther into the room. Mark stepped up behind to hear what the doctor had to say.

"How is she?" Scott asked.

The doctor smiled at the baby before he glanced

up at Kate. "She's fine. Just a few scrapes and bruises. She'll be sore for a few days. It could have been a lot worse if it hadn't been for Mr. Webber here. He saved Betsy's life."

The three turned and stared at Mark. "You didn't tell us you were the hero," Brock said.

Mark shrugged. "I wasn't. Just lucky I was close enough I could get to her."

"That's not the way Betsy told it." Doc Hunter's eyes twinkled, and he motioned for them to follow him. "She'll want to see all of you. So come on back."

When they stepped into the treatment room, Betsy sat on the edge of an exam table. Her legs dangled over the side, and big bandages covered both knees. Her mouth curled down in a frown when she saw them, and she wagged a finger at Mark. "I thought you gave me a choice of bringing me here or calling my family."

Mark grinned. "I did. But I had a choice, too. I knew Scott and Brock would want to break my neck if I didn't tell them what happened. And now that I've met Kate, I think she could be worse than either of them."

Kate wrapped her arm around her sister's shoulder and smiled at him. "You've got that right. My sister is very special to me."

Scott lifted Betsy's hands to look at the medicine covering the scrapes. "You had a close call.

You need to be careful when you walk out into the street from now on."

Mark gave a discreet cough, and they all turned to stare at him. "I've been thinking about this while I've been waiting, and I have some questions about what happened. I don't think this was a random incident. I think somebody deliberately tried to run Betsy down."

"What?" Kate's voice almost shrieked.

"That car came out of nowhere and headed right toward her. I didn't think I could get to her in time, but I did."

Kate leaned against the exam table, and tears flooded her eyes. "Then thank you, Mr. Webber, for saving my sister's life."

"It wasn't as bad as that," Betsy insisted. "It probably was some teenagers speeding. You know how crazy they drive on the island sometimes."

Mark took a deep breath. "There's something else I didn't tell you because I wanted Betsy to tell all of you at the same time."

"What is it?" Kate asked.

Betsy frowned. "I don't know what you're talking about."

"The phone call. Tell them about the phone call."

Betsy looked away. "I told you it was a wrong number."

Mark shook his head. "It's too much of a coincidence, Betsy. You receive a strange phone call and minutes later you're almost run down in the street. It may be connected."

Kate's eyes grew wide, and she tightened her arm around Betsy. "What about a phone call?"

For the next few minutes, Betsy told them everything she remembered about the raspy voice on her cell phone. "I really did think it was a wrong number," she insisted.

"And you're sure he said 'where is it?'"

"That's what he said. I have no idea what he was talking about."

Everyone was quiet for a moment as they digested this new information. After a moment, Kate spoke. "You shouldn't stay alone, Betsy. I'll take Emma to our house, and I want you to move into Treasury's bed-and-breakfast for a few days."

"That's ridiculous. I'll be fine at home."

Scott shook his head. "No, that house is too isolated, and you're not staying out there alone with Emma. If you won't consider your safety, at least think of our little sister. You already have your studio at Treasury's. That would be the perfect place for you."

"Scott and Kate are right. You need to go to Treasury's and stay there until we can determine if the two incidents are related," Brock added.

"But, Scott, you're off tomorrow, and you promised to take me out on Pamlico Sound in the morning during low tide," Betsy protested. "I need to get some pictures of the waterfowl in the marshes along the coast. Can we still do that?"

Scott and Kate looked at each other, and she gave a small nod. "Okay," he said. "I'll pick you up in the morning about five-thirty."

"Good. I'll be expecting you."

Mark's stomach knotted with dread. He jammed his fists in the pockets of his jeans and rocked back on his heels. "There's something I should tell you before you decide about staying at the bed-and-breakfast."

Her eyes grew large. "What is it?"

He exhaled sharply. "I'm already staying there. You may not feel comfortable having me close by, but with me at the same place I can keep an eye on you. Then we can determine if there's a danger to you or not."

Her expression grew dark, and he wondered how deep her hatred for him went. Had her experience in Memphis made her so angry she would refuse the protection of a federal DEA agent? He hoped not.

Kate touched Betsy's arm, and she turned to stare at her sister. "Betsy, we couldn't bear it if something happened to you. No matter what happened between you and Mark in the past, I'll feel better knowing there's someone watching out for you."

Betsy's eyes softened, and she squeezed her sister's hand. "All right. I'll go to Treasury's if it will make all of you feel better." She took a deep breath and hopped to the floor. "Doc Hunter told me I was free to leave. So if someone will drive me back to my truck, I'll go home and pack some clothes."

Scott laid a restraining hand on her arm. "Oh, no you won't. Brock and I will take care of the truck." He turned to Mark. "Do you mind taking Betsy home to get her clothes then driving her to Treasury's?"

Mark nodded. "I'll be glad to do that."

Brock and Scott followed Betsy out the door of the exam room, but Kate turned to block Mark from exiting. "Mr. Webber, I've been a police officer ever since I graduated from college. Even though I'm on leave now with my baby, I'm still involved in ongoing investigations on the island. I also understand how people who've been hurt by investigations don't always understand an officer's reasons for what they did." She wrapped her arms around her baby and stared intently at him. "I've never judged you as an officer, only as a man who professed to be a friend to my sister. I hope you won't do anything else while you're here to add to her hurt."

Mark's face burned from the scrutiny of Kate's eyes. "We're dealing with some desperate criminals, Mrs. Gentry, and I'm afraid Betsy has attracted their attention. I only want to make sure she remains safe."

"I'm glad you're concerned for her safety. I'll feel better knowing an officer is at Treasury's."

"I'll watch out for her," he promised.

Kate nodded, bit down on her lip, and led Mark down the hallway of the health center to the parking lot where the others waited. He could see the flicker of concern in all their faces, and none of them spoke as he climbed into the car and cranked the engine.

During the last few minutes, his assignment had become more complicated. Brock and Scott were right when they said he should have passed up an assignment on the island where Betsy grew up. He'd never expected to be involved with her whole family, but now he was.

After getting directions from Betsy, he pulled into the street on his way to her house. She sat in the passenger seat and didn't speak but gazed out the window as they passed through the village streets jammed with tourists. He darted a glance at her every so often, but she didn't look at him.

He wondered what she was thinking. Did she regret agreeing to stay in the same bed-and-breakfast where he was a guest? If she did, he'd have to prove to her he didn't mean to cause her any problems. After all, he was on Ocracoke to do a job, and he intended to close this assignment like he had so many others in the past.

Before that happened, though, he had to make sure the men he was after hadn't decided Betsy had something they wanted. He'd dealt with their kind before. Human life held little meaning for them, and their enemies often found themselves facing quick retribution.

He was determined that wouldn't happen to Betsy.

FOUR

All the way to her house, Betsy's mind whirled with everything that had happened since she left home this morning. All she'd wanted when she went to Springer's Point was to observe the white ibises and sooty terns that frequented the area. Seeing a man die hadn't been part of the plan.

In fact her whole day had turned into something she might expect to see in an action flick. No matter how much she might protest, the incident with the speeding car troubled her, but it didn't even compare with the distress she'd experienced at coming face-to-face with Mark Webber. She'd convinced herself she would never see him again, but she'd been wrong.

Now she was about to take refuge at Treasury's bed-and-breakfast, where she would be reminded every day of how he'd deceived her in the past. She didn't want to relive that time in her life, but with Mark's presence at the inn, there didn't seem to be a way around it. Not with her family insisting she wasn't safe at home.

Mark turned the car onto the road leading to her house, and she glanced at him. He hadn't said anything since they left the health center. Did he regret agreeing to watch out for her? She crossed her arms and frowned. Of course he did. He wouldn't let anything interfere with his investigation. Not even her safety.

When he pulled the car to a stop, she jumped out and was already unlocking the front door before he caught up with her. "What's the hurry?" he asked.

She shrugged and pushed the door open. "No reason." She stepped into the living room and motioned toward the sofa. "You can have a seat there. I'll pack some clothes and be back in a few minutes."

"You need any help?"

She shook her head. "No, thanks."

Betsy hurried into her bedroom, closed the door and leaned against it. She took a deep breath and tried to calm her racing heartbeat. Her skin prickled just as it had done when the speeding car had raced past her. Mark had saved her life, and she had to admit she was thankful he was there.

She might have reservations about Mark as a person, but she knew he was good at his job. If someone did want to hurt her, she could do worse than have Mark Webber protecting her. Until they determined whether she was in danger, she would have to make the best of a bad situation and accept his help. With a sigh, she jerked the closet door open and began to pull out some clothes.

Fifteen minutes later, Betsy pulled her rolling suitcase into the living room. Mark rose from the couch and came toward her. "I'll put that in my car for you."

She smiled. "Thanks."

His eyes crinkled at the corners. "No, thank you."

"For what?"

"For smiling. That's the first time I've seen a glimpse of the Betsy I once knew since we met at Springer's Point this morning. I always thought you had a beautiful smile."

His words stirred a warning in her, and she frowned. "I'm not the naive girl I was then, Mark. I've discovered that you can't trust some people, and it's better to be wary before becoming close to someone."

He exhaled and reached for the handle of her suitcase. "I'm sorry if I caused you to be cynical about people, Betsy. Your acceptance of everyone was one of the things I liked most about you."

She jerked the suitcase away and glared at him. "Did you think that because I chose to see the good in people I would keep quiet about illegal activities like drug dealing?"

Mark glanced down at her hand clutching the handle of the rolling bag and flexed his fingers. "I told myself you wouldn't, but you were always telling me how great Mr. Rousseau was and what a terrific boss he was. I could tell he was interested in you. I had to know if you were involved with him."

Even after all these years, the hurt she'd felt when she found out Mark had used her to crack a case resurfaced, and tears threatened to spill from her eyes. "Well, you were wrong. I was just a girl from a remote island who'd never been away from home, and I thought you were my friend. All I was to you was a means to an end."

The muscle in his jaw twitched. "That's not true. I had a job to do, and I did it. You weren't even arrested."

"No. I suppose I have your fellow officers to thank for that. Everybody else involved in the case knew right away I wasn't involved. It was almost as if you were on some kind of mission to get the bad guys and it didn't matter who ended up getting hurt."

"I was on a mission, but I didn't mean to hurt you," he insisted. "I called dozens of times afterward, but you wouldn't listen to what I had to say."

Mark's dark eyes flickered, and for a moment Betsy thought she detected a hint of sadness. She took a deep breath and shook her head. "This is getting us nowhere. We may never agree on what happened in Memphis. For now, though, it looks like we may be seeing quite a bit of each other for a while. Let's try to make the best of it."

He nodded. "You're right. Think of me as a cop who's on assignment and wants to make sure a potential witness doesn't get hurt."

Potential witness? The words jabbed at her heart like knife pricks. History was repeating itself. He'd once viewed her as an opportunity to break a case, and now he saw her in the same way. She'd been right about him. He didn't care about anybody or anything except whatever case he was working on.

She blinked back tears and lifted her chin. "I guess some things never change."

His eyes grew wide. "Betsy, I didn't mean..."

Her ringing cell phone interrupted her. She jerked it from her fanny pack and pressed it to her ear. "Hello."

"Hello, Miss Michaels. How's your day going so far?"

A chill flowed through Betsy at the raspy voice she'd heard once before when she thought it was a wrong number. This time, he'd called her by name. "W-Who is this?"

"Just a friend checking in to see how you're holding up."

Her hand shook, and her eyes grew wide. Mark frowned and stepped closer. His mouth formed a silent *what?*

Betsy pulled the phone away from her ear, clicked to speaker phone, and held it out so they both could hear. "What do you want?"

A low chuckle rattled into the room. "Something you have."

"I don't know what you're talking about." Betsy's hand shook, and Mark's fingers tightened around hers to hold the phone still.

"Don't play me for an idiot. He gave it to you."

Betsy swallowed to relieve her burning throat, but her mouth had gone dry. "Nobody gave anything to me."

"Oh, really? I find that hard to believe. I think you want to bargain with me. Okay, I'll play along. How much do you want for it?"

"I'm telling you I have no idea what you're talking about." Her shrill words bounced off the walls.

For a moment he didn't speak. Then he sighed, and the sound seeped into her soul like an icy death knell. "Have it your way, Miss Michaels. But I think you've just made the wrong choice."

"W-what do you mean?"

"The car at the cemetery was just a warning. You'd better keep looking behind you, because we're coming for you. When we do, you'll wish you'd cooperated with us."

"Please, listen to me…"

The silence on the phone told her the caller had disconnected. The cell phone slipped through her fingers and thudded to the floor at her feet. Mark bent down, scooped it up, and handed it back to her.

"We'll check the phone records, Betsy. I'll find out who called."

She bit her lip and shook her head. "You forget I've lived my whole life with police officers. I know he was smart enough to use a phone that can't be traced."

He reached out and gripped her hand. "You're probably right, but we'll try anyway. Until we know who he is, I'll stay close to you. I promise I'll protect you."

Betsy glanced down at their locked hands. A few minutes ago, he'd held her fingers still when the voice on the phone had frightened her. In that moment she'd been glad Mark was with her, and she felt the same way now.

The memory of what had occurred in Memphis was nothing compared to what she had experienced today. Mark hadn't given up until he'd brought that case to a close, and he hadn't changed. His dogged persistence would make him do everything in his power to keep her safe and to find out who had called. If he could do that, it would make spending time with him worthwhile.

Fifteen minutes later, Mark followed Betsy through the back door of the Island Connection Bed-and-Breakfast. He hadn't known Betsy had a studio in the house when he'd booked his reservation. Maybe it would have been better if he had stayed somewhere else, but then he wouldn't have been able to watch out for Betsy.

He shook his head in resignation. This might not be what he'd envisioned when he came to the island, but he had to admit he looked forward to seeing Betsy on a regular basis. He had never meant to hurt her, and it pained him greatly that he'd done just that. Truth was, even when he was so intent on bringing down Rousseau, he knew Betsy had qualities he admired.

Why couldn't he see the good in people the way she did? There were two reasons. The first was because she had a deep faith in God. He'd never known anyone like her. She'd often spoken to him and tried to convince him of God's love, but he'd never been able to accept something he couldn't see.

The other reason was because he'd seen what human beings can do to each other, and it sickened him. He'd never wanted to spend his life searching for hardened criminals who gave no thought to the hurt they inflicted on their victims, but that's just what he'd done. And all because of that long-ago morning in his family's driveway. He couldn't forget the vow he'd made that day.

Now, eighteen years later, he couldn't rid himself of the obsession that had ruled his life ever since. He'd put a lot of criminals behind bars, but he'd left behind some innocent victims along the way. Betsy was one of them, and he regretted that more than she would ever know.

Betsy walked into the kitchen of the bed-and-breakfast and he trailed close behind. Treasury Wilkes, the elderly owner he'd met when he first arrived, bustled through the door from the dining room. Her eyebrows drew down in a worried expression. "Land sakes, Betsy. Kate came by and told me what happened to you today." She stopped in front of Betsy, grasped her arms and stared into her face. "Are you all right, darling?"

Betsy smiled and leaned over to plant a kiss on Treasury's cheek. "I'm fine." She straightened and glanced over her shoulder at Mark. "I know you've met Treasury, but you may not know she's been a second mother to my sisters and me ever since our mother died."

He pulled Betsy's rolling bag to a stop and nodded. "You said your studio was here, but I didn't realize the close tie between the two of you."

Treasury's eyes twinkled, and she put her arm

around Betsy's shoulders. "Oh my, yes. Kate, Betsy and Emma are the daughters I never had." A smile pulled at her lips. "And speaking of Emma, we spent the morning at the beach and had a great time. Kate took her home with her. Emma was really excited that she's going to help take care of the baby for a few days."

Betsy's forehead wrinkled, and Mark detected a brief flicker of fear in her eyes. "Did Kate tell you why?"

"She said the incident at Springer's Point had upset you, and you were going to stay close to your studio for a few days." She smiled at Mark. "And that Mr. Webber is going to keep an eye on you to make sure you do."

Betsy darted a glance at Mark, and he chuckled. "I'll try to do that, Mrs. Wilkes, but Betsy can be strong-willed at times."

"Call me Treasury." With a knowing look she directed a piercing gaze at him. "You sound like you know Betsy."

Betsy nodded and reached for her suitcase. "Mark and I knew each other when I was in Memphis. I'll tell you about it later. Now I need to unpack these clothes and do some work on the painting I'm sending to the gallery on the mainland."

Treasury glanced at the clock above the kitchen stove and tapped her chin. "You'll have plenty of time to paint before dinner. I'm not cooking for any of my guests tonight. So it'll just be the three of us. We can eat on the back porch about six o'clock. Is that all right with the two of you?"

Mark frowned and shook his head. "You don't have to include me in dinner if none of the other guests are eating. I can get something somewhere else."

Treasury waved her hand in dismissal and chuckled. "Nonsense. If you're going to watch after my girl, I want you around all the time. I'm sure Betsy does, too." She glanced at Betsy. "Is that right?"

Mark detected a slight hesitation before Betsy replied. "Of course you should join us, Mark. After all you won't find better food on the island."

He stared into Betsy's eyes and tried to sense a hint of truth in her words, but her stony gaze gave away nothing. After a moment, he nodded. "Okay, ladies. I'll see you at six. Now, Betsy, I'll take your bag to your studio if you'll lead the way."

Betsy whirled and hurried from the kitchen with him right behind. They didn't speak as she led him up the stairs and to the room at the end of hall. When she opened the door and stepped inside, he followed and rolled her bag into the room. She motioned toward a spot next to a small bed that sat against one wall.

"You can leave the bag there."

He placed the bag at the spot she indicated and glanced around the large room. Sunlight poured through two windows and lit the easel sitting in front of them. A computer, sketch pads and several stacks of photographs covered the top of a desk on the opposite wall, but it was the ceramic mug with a Degas painting stamped on it that caught his attention. An assortment of pens and pencils along with a pair of scissors stuck out of the top.

He picked it up and studied the imprinted artwork and glanced at Betsy. "*The Rehearsal* by Edgar Degas. I've always liked this painting."

Her eyes grew wide. "I can't believe you recognized it."

Mark chuckled and placed the mug back on the desk. "Contrary to what you might think, Betsy, I graduated from college, and I happened to take some art classes while I was there. Degas is one of my favorite artists. I like the way he conveys movement." He gave the cup a gentle shake and smiled at the rattle of the pencils and scissors inside. "I wonder what Degas would think about his painting decorating the side of a pencil holder?"

"I can't believe you're an art lover." Betsy tilted her head to one side and arched an eyebrow. "You never mentioned any of that before."

"I guess I never thought it was important." He

glanced at his watch and headed toward the door. "I'd better go so you can get to work. I'll see you at dinner."

He stepped into the hall but stopped when she called out to him. When he turned, he saw she had followed him to the door. She took a deep breath and licked her lips.

"Mark," she said, "thank you for everything you've done for me today. I'm afraid I haven't been as nice as I could have been. My mother always told me it's better to guard your words than say something you regret. I hope you'll forgive me for some of the things I said."

His heart thudded at her words, and he took a step toward her. "Don't worry about it, Betsy. I understand how you feel, but I'm not really as bad as you think. Maybe while I'm here we can get to know each other better and become friends again."

She gave a slight nod. "Maybe so. I'm beginning to think there's a lot about you I don't know."

"I'll see you at dinner," he mumbled before he turned and strode down the hall toward his room.

When he reached his door, he glanced back, but she had already disappeared into her studio. He groaned and pushed into his room. After sinking down on the bed, he scrubbed a hand across his face. Seeing Betsy today had brought back a lot of memories. When she left Memphis, he thought he could put her and the hurt he'd caused her out of his mind, but he knew he never had.

Now, it looked like they would be spending a lot of time together in the next few weeks, and he didn't know how he would handle it. He'd known when he first met her she was special, but he'd tried to deny it. Seeing her where she'd grown up and with her family only confirmed what he'd worked to forget.

The truth flashed in his mind, and he groaned again. His feelings hadn't changed in the years since he'd last seen her. He was just as attracted to her now as he had been then. But something else hadn't changed, either. He would never act on his feelings for her.

All he wanted was to solve his latest case and get back to the mainland as quickly as possible. There were other investigations waiting for him, and a woman like Betsy Michaels had no place in the life he had chosen.

FIVE

The candle on Treasury's back porch wicker table flickered in the gentle breeze that blew across the sandy yard. Overhead stars twinkled in the sky. Betsy couldn't recall a more beautiful night. Ever since she and Mark had arrived at Treasury's house earlier, she'd worried about having dinner with him, but it had really gone well.

Maybe Treasury's presence had helped. She had been happy to give Mark a history of the island she'd lived on all her life, and he had listened as she told the stories of how her home had withstood years of hurricanes. The conversation hadn't interfered with Mark's appetite, though. She hadn't seen anyone eat as much as Mark had since the first time her brother, Scott, sat down at Treasury's table when he came to the island.

Betsy took a sip from her coffee cup and stared over the rim at Mark, who scraped the last bite of Treasury's fig cake from his dessert plate and plopped it in his mouth. His lips curved into a half smile, as if to confirm the look of satisfaction in his eyes.

"Did you enjoy your meal?" Betsy tried to keep from smirking.

A slow flush spread over Mark's face, and he wiped at the grin on his face with his napkin. "I did. It's been a long time since I've eaten anything as good." He glanced around. "Where did Mrs. Wilkes go? I need to thank her for dinner."

Betsy reached across the table, picked up his dessert plate, and set it on hers. "She went inside while you were absorbed in devouring your cake. I told her I'd bring the dishes when we finished."

He glanced over his shoulder at the back door and shook his head. "I can't believe I was so pre-occupied. I'll catch her later and tell her how much I enjoyed the meal."

Betsy arched an eyebrow. "Oh, I think she knows."

"She's a very special lady, and I can tell she loves you a lot."

Betsy smiled. "She means the world to me. My mother died when I was sixteen. Kate had just graduated from college, and Emma was four. Treasury became our second mother and helped us through a rough time. Then when our father died, we became even closer."

"I remember you talking about your family, but

they were just names. Now that I've met them I realize how fortunate you are to have them."

Betsy settled back in her chair and crossed her arms over her stomach. "I am truly blessed. When Mom died, Kate took over her role in our family. She and Brock were engaged at the time, but Kate decided she had a responsibility to her family. They ended their engagement and went their separate ways. When Brock came back here a few years ago, they realized they'd never quit loving each other." She looked reflective for a moment. "Kate's on leave right now from the sheriff's office with the baby, but I doubt she'll ever go back. She's happy to be at home with Brock and her son."

"They look like the picture of a happy family. What about Scott? You seem close to him."

Betsy nodded. "He's the big brother I always dreamed of having. His mother was our dad's first wife. She died when Scott was born, and her sister took him and disappeared. My father searched for years. Right before Dad died, he made Kate promise we'd keep looking." Her voice filled with emotion. "A private investigator friend of Brock's found him. He had just left the military and was suffering from post-traumatic stress disorder when he came here. Finding the family he'd always wanted and falling in love with Lisa helped him face his tortured past."

"All of you seem happy now."

"We are. We're all content with our lives and wouldn't change anything."

"I'm glad you're happy, Betsy." Mark stared at her a moment before he pushed to his feet and reached for the dishes. "I'll take these in."

Betsy watched in silence as he juggled the stack of dirty dishes and entered the house. Tonight she'd felt comfortable talking with Mark, and it troubled her. She sprang to her feet and walked to the railing that enclosed the back porch. She wrapped her fingers around the banister and gazed across the backyard. The sweet tones of the wind chime hanging at the other end of the porch drifted across the quiet night. Betsy tipped her head back, closed her eyes, and inhaled.

"What are you thinking?"

She sensed his presence even before the soft tone of Mark's voice washed over her. Suddenly nervous, she gripped the railing to keep from turning to face him. "I love the peaceful nights on the island."

He moved to stand beside her and placed his hands on the railing next to hers. "I remember how you used to talk about how beautiful your island was. Now I see what you meant."

Her heart fluttered, but she spoke with a stiff upper lip. "Don't do that, Mark."

He turned to stare at her. "What?"

"Don't bring up what we said to each other. It's all in the past, and we need to keep it there."

He exhaled. "Okay. I didn't mean anything by what I said. I was just making conversation."

She pushed back from the railing and turned to face him. "I'm sorry. I shouldn't have said that. I'll try not to read something into everything you say. After all, you didn't have to offer to keep an eye on me. I hope you don't feel like my family forced you."

He shook his head. "I don't think that. I don't want anything bad to happen to you." He shrugged. "But who knows? We may be all wrong about this. Those phone calls may have nothing to do with what happened at Springer's Point."

"You don't believe that any more than I do."

His white teeth flashed behind his lazy smile. "Maybe not, but I thought it might make you feel better."

She wrapped her arms around her waist to control the shudder coursing through her body. "I don't think I'll feel better until we know who tried to run me down,"

"I won't give up until I find out who it was."

His words, meant to console her, only added to her conflicting emotions. If there was one thing she knew about Mark Webber...it was that once he had a goal in mind he didn't waver. She also knew the last time she'd crossed his path she had ended up as a victim in his desire to see justice done. She couldn't let that happen again.

She stepped back from the railing and peered up at him. "I know you won't. I've seen you work before. This time I'm just glad I'm not the one you're after."

His eyes hardened and he spoke through gritted teeth. "I'm sorry I hurt you, Betsy. I promise I won't do it again. After this case is over, I'll leave on the first ferry out of here, and you won't ever have to lay eyes on me again. Until then, it looks like we may be spending a lot of time together, and I'm getting tired of defending my past actions. I'd like to call a truce for now. Can you do that?"

The truth of his words sent a flood of remorse through her. Had she tried to make Mark feel guilty by reminding him of their past connection? If so, she needed to concentrate on why he was here and the reason she needed him in her life right now. She took a deep breath.

"Consider it done. I won't bring the past up again as long as you're here."

"Good. Now why don't we go inside? It's been a busy day, and I'm beat." He walked to the back door and held it open for her. "I'll walk you to your room."

She slipped past him into the house. The sound of his footsteps behind gave her a feeling of security as she climbed the stairs to her studio. When they arrived at the door, she turned and smiled. "I enjoyed having dinner with you tonight, Mark. And I'm glad we were able to talk afterward."

He shoved his hands in his pockets and rocked back on his heels. "Me, too."

She pushed the door open but stopped before entering her room and turned to face him. "As you know, Scott is taking me out in the boat tomorrow morning so I can take some pictures of the waterfowl feeding. Would you like to tag along?"

She could hardly believe she had invited him, but for some reason she really wanted him to come.

"I'd like that." His soft words flowed over her.

She cocked her head to one side and grinned. "We're leaving at five-thirty. Think you can get up that early?"

A tiny smirk pulled at his lips. "I'm an early riser. I'll meet you in the kitchen at five-fifteen."

"Good. I'll see you then."

He reached out and touched her arm as she took a step to enter the room, and she halted. He moved closer and gazed into her eyes. "I don't know what the next few days will be like, but I promise I'll always be here for you."

"I appreciate that, Mark." She shrugged. "And who knows…maybe whoever phoned me will discover I don't have what they want and will leave me alone."

"Maybe, but we can't count on it. I'll see you in the morning. Sleep well."

"You, too."

She went into her room and closed the door. The lamp she'd left burning on the bedside table cast a beam of light across her desk and the painting on the easel. With a gasp she realized she hadn't drawn the curtains before she went downstairs. She had no idea what anyone watching from outside could see through the second floor windows, but she wasn't taking any chances.

She rushed across the room and pulled down the shades. As she turned back toward the bed, she noticed her fanny pack lying on her desk where she'd placed it earlier and remembered she hadn't taken her cell phone out. She unzipped the pouch and began to pull out the items she'd stuck inside this morning.

Her cell phone was the first. She smiled at how the painted flowers and butterflies on the phone's cover had amused Mark, then pulled out the small camera she'd carried with her to the Point. As she stuck her hand back inside for the notepad she used to jot down descriptions, her fingers brushed against two pens.

She pulled both of them out and stared at them for a moment. The silver one with the logo for The Coffee Cup she remembered placing inside, but the other one, a sleek, black ballpoint pen, didn't look familiar. She searched her mind for where she might have gotten it.

After a moment, she smiled and nodded. It looked like the pens the bank had on the table where they kept deposit slips. She must have picked it up when she was in there last week. She shoved the two pens into the mug with the Degas painting imprint and plugged her phone into its charger.

An hour later, Betsy sat at her desk reading her Bible. She finished reading the words that spoke of forgiveness, closed the book and placed it on the shelf above. The words brought to mind her mother, who had always taught her to forgive others. She thought of Mark and how she'd harbored anger against him for years. Perhaps she had been too quick to judge him.

She understood the pressures placed on law enforcement officers because she had seen it with her sister, brother and brother-in-law. At the time she'd known Mark, he must have been under a lot of stress to close a case, and she needed to quit thinking he'd deliberately set out to hurt her. In the coming days, she needed to remind herself of how her mother would expect her to offer forgiveness when someone said they were sorry.

With a sigh, she pushed up from her desk and walked to her bed. She sat down on the edge of the mattress and slipped her shoes off. As she started to lie down, her gaze drifted across the mug holding her pens and pencils. She smiled at how surprised she'd been when Mark recognized the painting imprinted on the container's side. Maybe there was another side to Mark she'd never seen. If so, it would be interesting to find out more.

She reached to turn off the lamp but hesitated. She glanced down at the goose bumps on her arms and pressed her hand against her pounding chest. Something wasn't right.

Betsy glanced around the room but she saw nothing to explain her sudden fear. She frowned and shook her head. She was being ridiculous. The events of the day really had taken a toll on her.

After a moment, she switched off the lamp and slipped beneath the covers. She drew the sheet up to her chin and stared at the ceiling. The darkness in the room closed around her like a silent cocoon. She lay still and hoped whatever had triggered her disturbing emotions would pass, but it didn't.

Thoughts of a man's lifeless body, a speeding car and a raspy voice on the phone flashed through her mind. She groaned, turned on her stomach, and pulled her pillow over her head. Even that didn't blot out her rising fear.

Then she thought of Mark who slept a few doors away from her, and her growing panic subsided. He had promised he would take care of her. Her body relaxed, and her heartbeat slowed. She pulled the pillow from over her head, pounded it with her fist and laid her head on it. A tranquil calm filled her, and she drifted into a peaceful sleep.

Mark had seen the sun rise many times during his life, but he didn't think he'd ever seen anything as beautiful as dawn breaking across Pamlico Sound. The sun first appeared like a tiny speck on the dark horizon, but within three minutes, its golden rays had radiated across the sky in a kaleidoscope of colors that announced a new day had arrived.

He sat hunched in the rigid-hulled boat Scott steered as they navigated the coastal shoreline. All around he heard the sounds of an awakening island. He spied several fishing boats on the horizon and knew they were carrying tourists out to deeper water for a day of deep-sea fishing. Gulls circled overhead, and in the distance he could see others perched on pilings along the coastline. Mark closed his eyes and inhaled the smell of the sea.

"Are you asleep?" Betsy's teasing voice brought him out of his daydreams.

"No, just enjoying the peaceful morning. You've been so busy snapping pictures, I didn't think you even knew Scott and I were with you."

She laughed and stretched her arms over her

head. "I knew you were here. Your snoring gave you away."

"Don't pay any attention to her, Mark," Scott said. "Betsy's in her own world out here. She loves to watch the birds we have on Ocracoke. On days I'm working she even comes out here and sits in one of the duck blinds to snap her photographs."

Mark pointed to a small box-like structure on stilts anchored in the water some distance from them. "Is that a blind over there?"

Betsy nodded. "Yeah, that's a stake blind." She handed Mark the binoculars she'd brought along. "Take a closer look at it and you can see the ladder where hunters tie their boats before they climb inside. They can stay in there for hours and hunt. I like to sit inside and photograph the ducks and geese feeding, but I don't come out during hunting season much. It upsets me too much to see all the beautiful birds that are killed."

"Hey, Betsy," Scott called out. "Why don't we show Mark the other place you like to hang out in for your photo shoots?"

"Fine with me."

Betsy took the camera from around her neck and put it back in its case as Scott turned the boat in a circle. The boat skimmed the water's surface as they headed out into deeper water. The early morning sun sparkled on Betsy's hair, wet from the saltwater spray, and excitement gleamed in her eyes.

She looked so different this morning from the girl he'd first met in Memphis. Back then, she was a young college student who had her sights set on an art career in the city. Now she was all grown up, happy and secure in her life as a painter of landscapes and wildlife on the island she loved. This woman at home on the water and along the salt marshes of Ocracoke bore little resemblance to the girl he'd known, and he liked this new and improved Betsy.

Shading her eyes with her hand, she squinted in the sun that now beat down on their heads and scanned the horizon. After about five minutes she pointed straight ahead. "There's one, Scott."

Her brother slowed the boat and let it drift for a minute or so before he came to a stop. The boat, its engine idling, bobbed up and down on the peaceful water. Mark looked all around but could see nothing except water in all directions.

He turned to Betsy and frowned. "What do you want to show me?"

Grinning, she threw her legs over the side of the boat and hopped in the water. To his surprise, she didn't sink. Instead she stood, the water lapping at her ankles, and laughed. She crooked her finger and motioned for him to join her. "Come on in. You won't drown."

He turned to Scott, who looked just as amused as Betsy. "I don't understand."

"I know how you feel," her brother said. "The first time I saw this I couldn't believe it."

Betsy leaned back into the boat and grabbed Mark's arm. "I'm standing on a submerged sandbar that's covered with a few inches of water. Get out and let me show you a curtain blind."

He climbed over the edge of the boat and joined Betsy. The water lapped at their ankles as she led him a few feet to a rectangular concrete structure built down into the sandbar. It looked like two men might easily fit inside. "This is a curtain blind," she said. "Hunters can climb down into this concrete box and be at eye level with the water, and the ducks can't see them."

"What's that?" He pointed to a wooden frame that circled the top of the box.

"That's a waterproof canvas curtain. The owner of the blind brings hunters out here at low tide and leaves them. As the tide rises, they just pull that curtain up to keep the water from pouring in."

Mark's eyes grew wide. "You mean they stay out this far from shore without a boat to get back?"

Betsy chuckled. "Yeah, but it's not dangerous. The owner of the blind picks them up at the end of the day. Hunters who use these blinds wouldn't hunt any other way. I understand hunting is a way of making a living for a lot of our islanders, but I hate to see our wildlife killed." She pointed across the water, and he turned to see a wooden frame with slats floating nearby. "See that? It's called a wing and is about sixteen by twenty-four feet with slats about eight inches apart. It's anchored away from the curtain right now, but in duck hunting season it's brought closer, and decoys are placed on the wooden slats. When the ducks or geese flying overhead see the decoys, they come toward them, and the hunters have a clear shot."

Mark gazed in the direction of the shoreline, but it wasn't visible from here. "I can't believe you stay out here alone."

She smiled. "This blind belongs to Milt Wilson. He brings me out here and comes back for me several hours later. I like spending time alone with the birds on the water and feel the breeze blowing salt water in my face. It brings me closer to God. I can feel his presence."

The contentment and happiness he saw on her face made him envy what she'd found in her life, and a desire like he'd never known burned in the pit of his stomach. He longed for what Betsy had, but he knew he'd never find it. His course in life had been determined a long time ago, and it couldn't be changed.

"I'm glad you brought me here, Betsy. It's given me another glimpse into who Betsy Michaels is now."

Her dark eyes narrowed. He thought she was going to respond, but after a moment she glanced back at her brother still in the boat. "Scott's waiting. We'd better go."

Mark followed her across the sandbar back to the boat. When they were inside, Scott turned toward shore, and Mark settled back in his seat. When Betsy had asked him to come along on the early morning trip, he'd agreed because he wanted to know more about what Betsy was like now. And he hadn't been disappointed in what he'd discovered.

What he was going to do about that was what had him worried. He had to keep reminding himself he had a job to do and not to get emotionally involved. Something told him that wasn't going to be easy.

SIX

Mark had enjoyed the time he spent with Betsy and Scott on Pamlico Sound earlier this morning, but the past few hours had proved to be a letdown. After extracting a promise from Betsy that she would stay in her studio until lunch, he'd left Treasury's house soon after their return to see if he could get a lead on the places John had frequented in the time he'd been on the island. A call to Brock had revealed they hadn't been able to track any of his movements, and hanging out for several hours at the various gathering places for island residents hadn't revealed anything, either.

Now, hungry and disappointed, he'd come back to the bed-and-breakfast to check on Betsy. He pushed through the back door into the kitchen and came to a stop as Betsy strolled in through the door from the dining room. When she saw him, she stopped and set down the plastic-covered canvas painting she held.

His heart did flip-flops just as it had done this

morning when he watched her photographing the wildlife she loved. It reminded him of how he used to feel when she'd glance at him across the dining room of the Memphis restaurant where they'd both worked. There was no denying the old attraction had overcome him again, but he wasn't going to give in. He took a deep breath and tried to return her smile.

"I'm back, just like I said." He pointed to his watch. "I said in time for lunch, and it's not even twelve yet."

She stepped into the kitchen and grinned at him. "Good timing. I just finished what I'd planned to do this morning."

He pointed to the painting she'd leaned against a kitchen chair. "Is that what you worked on?"

A chuckle rumbled in her throat. "Oh, no. The painting I worked on this morning is drying. This is one I finished a few weeks ago. I need to drop it off at Will Cardwell's studio. He's a potter, and we transport our work to a mainland gallery together. We have a shipment going out in a few days." She glanced his way. "Do you mind giving me a ride over there since my family has seen fit to make sure I can't leave here on my own?"

A coy smile pulled at her lips and the sight of her almost took his breath. His gaze raked her from her long, chestnut hair pulled back in a ponytail past the dimples that winked at him and on to the smile that lit her dark eyes. It ended at the paint-splattered, loose-fitting smock covering the jeans and T-shirt she wore. Even with the smudge on her forehead, she was still the most beautiful woman he'd ever seen.

He let out a long breath. "I'll be glad to take you anywhere you need to go. Then we'll get some lunch."

She reached back and tightened the rubber band holding her hair in place. "I felt safe this morning because I didn't think anybody would know we were out on the Sound. But what about in the middle of the day? Do you think we should go out now?"

"We'll stay where there are lots of people. The more people around, the safer it'll be."

She looked down at the clothes she was wearing. "I can't go looking like this. I'll be back in a few minutes." She started to leave but turned back. "Treasury needs some things from the Island General Store. It'll save her a trip if we stop by and pick them up before we come back. Do you mind?"

He nodded. "Sure. We can do that. I'll wait out back for you."

She beamed. "Good. Be back as soon as I change."

Fifteen minutes later Betsy walked out the back door of the house and headed toward Mark. He pushed up from leaning against the car's fender and studied her as she approached. Most women relied on makeup to enhance their beauty, but Betsy didn't need it. The touch of light-colored lipstick she'd applied looked just right for her. A square-shaped amethyst stone encircled with small diamonds dangled on a silver chain at the base of her throat. He remembered seeing her wear it every day when they worked at the restaurant in Memphis.

Betsy stopped next to him and wrinkled her forehead. "What's the matter?"

He pointed to her necklace. "I remember seeing you wear that in Memphis."

She nodded. "My mother gave it to me for my birthday not long before she died. It's my favorite piece of jewelry. I don't wear it as much as I used to, but I put it on today."

His gaze drifted over her, and a grin tugged at his mouth as he reached for the painting she held. "I notice you got rid of the smudge on your forehead. You clean up real nice."

"I'll take that as a compliment, mister."

"That's the way it was intended, ma'am."

"In that case, I'll let you buy me lunch. I've been working all morning and I'm starved." Betsy opened the back door of the car and settled the painting between the front and backseats. "There, that should do it." She slammed the door. "Let's drop this off first, then we can go eat. By the way, where are you taking me?"

"How about The Coffee Cup? It should be crowded with locals. If you see any strangers, you can let me know."

"Okay. But I warn you...that's the hangout for Grady Teach. If he's there and sees you with me, he'll want to know all about you. He calls himself the island historian, but he's really our biggest gossip."

Mark chuckled and opened the passenger door for her. "I saw him holding court there this morning. He's quite a colorful character. I heard him say he's a descendant of Blackbeard."

"He is, and he'll tell anyone who will listen all about it. His stories about Blackbeard's treasure that's still buried on the island sends tourists out to the salt marshes trying to find it."

Mark closed the door and walked to the driver's side. He slid behind the wheel and swiveled to face Betsy. "Do you think he might know anything about John? Maybe he ran into him somewhere on the island."

"It's worth a try."

He reached for the ignition and then drew back his hand. "Betsy, you seem different today. You're not as defensive as you were yesterday, and you seem more at ease."

A flush rose in her cheeks, and she clasped her

hands in her lap. "I decided I had to put the past out of my mind for the time being. I appreciate what you're trying to do for me, and I don't want to appear ungrateful. I hope you can forgive me for my snippy attitude yesterday. It won't happen again."

His eyebrows arched. Betsy was asking for his forgiveness? He never thought he'd hear those words from her. Then he remembered she'd said she would put the past out of her mind for the time being.

His good mood suddenly deflated. She might be trying to appear more cordial, but he had no doubt when this case was over they would be right back where they'd been before. All her old resentful feelings would return. Gritting his teeth, he put the car in gear and pulled out of the bed-and-breakfast parking lot.

"Tell me how to get to this studio where we're taking the painting."

She pointed to the right. "Go this way, and turn right at the second street. The studio is on the left."

Mark followed her directions, and a few minutes later pulled to a stop in front of a rustic, two-story house. A porch wrapped around two sides of the building, and a sign that said Cardwell's Studio and Gallery hung over the front door.

Wicker rockers sat on the porch, and several patrons appeared to be enjoying a relaxing moment.

Betsy jumped from the car and pulled her painting from the backseat. "The gallery where Will and I sell our pieces is through the front door. The studio where he teaches and works is around back. Let's go there first."

She led him along a path that circled the house and ended at a long, narrow building that sat at a ninety-degree angle from the house. She pushed a door open and stepped into the structure.

A gray-haired man stood at one end of the room where four women and two men sat, their bodies bent over pottery wheels. The man stopped beside one woman and patted her shoulder. "You're going to get the hang of this, Mary Lou. Like I say, it takes practice, practice, practice."

"That's Will Cardwell," Betsy whispered. "This is one of his beginner classes."

Will turned and smiled when he spotted her. "Betsy, what are you doing here today?"

She held up the canvas in her hand. "I brought another painting I want to include in the shipment to the mainland."

"Then put it in the back room with the others. If you decide to send anything else, have it here by Tuesday at noon. The truck will leave on the last ferry of the day on its way to Raleigh." His gaze landed on Mark, and he stepped forward with his hand extended. "I don't think we've met. I'm Will Cardwell."

"I'm Mark Webber, a friend of Betsy's." Mark shook the man's hand.

Will smiled. "Good to meet you, Mark. Are you a visitor to our island?"

"I am. Betsy had told me how beautiful it was, and I decided to see for myself."

Will's eyebrows arched, and he stroked his short, gray beard. "So, where do you live?"

"I'm originally from Memphis. I met Betsy when she was in school there. At present I'm living in Raleigh." He let his gaze wander over the people at the potter's wheels. "I've always wanted to be able to throw a pot. Even took a course in school, but I'm afraid I didn't show much promise."

Will laughed and glanced toward his students. "It's really not as hard as it looks. I'd be glad to show you while you're on the island."

Mark shook his head. "I'm more into wood carving. In fact, I used to do a lot of it."

"You used to do a lot of what?"

He glanced around at Betsy who had re-entered the room and stopped beside him. He waved his hand in dismissal. "Oh, it's nothing."

"He was just telling me he likes wood carving," Will said.

Betsy's eyes grew wide. "You never told me that."

"It's only a hobby." Mark's face grew warm.

Will glanced back at his students and grinned. "It looks like Mary Lou is about to have a meltdown. I'd better check on her." He nodded to Mark. "It's good to meet you, Mark. Have Betsy show you around the gallery before you leave. She has some great work on display there. You might even want to buy one."

Betsy laughed and swatted at Will's arm. "Don't put him on the spot, Will. I'm sure Mark would rather spend his money on something besides a painting of mine."

Will chuckled and turned to leave. He'd only taken a few steps when he whirled and came back. "I just had a thought. Since Mark likes wood carving, you should take him by Luke Butler's studio. He might really enjoy seeing the decoys Luke carves."

"Decoys?" The word caught Mark's attention.

Will nodded. "He's a master at carving decoys. You wouldn't believe how many hunters collect hand-carved decoys."

"I'd like to see some of his work," Mark said.

Betsy crossed her arms and cocked an eyebrow.

"I thought you were going to buy me lunch at The Coffee Cup and then pick up Treasury's list of items at the Island General Store."

Will laughed and backed away. "You'd better take this girl and get her something to eat. She gets mean when she's hungry."

Mark nodded. "I see what you mean. Let's go, Betsy. We can go to the wood carver's studio later."

When they were back in the car, Betsy swiveled in her seat and faced Mark. "Do you really want to go to Luke's studio now?"

He shook his head and pulled into the street. "No. We can eat first, but it struck me as strange when Will mentioned there's a man on the island who carves decoys."

Her frown dissolved into a look of surprise. "The man at Springer's Point mentioned decoys. Do you think Luke's decoys could be related to the drug-smuggling ring in some way?"

"I don't know. Does he ship any to the mainland, or does he sell from his shop?"

"He has several places he sends them. Do you think he might be smuggling drugs inside some of them?"

"It's possible. I want to see his studio. As soon as we eat, you can take me there."

Betsy shook her head and stared out the window.

"Luke Butler involved in a drug-smuggling ring? I can't believe it. He's such a nice man."

Mark didn't reply. He was too busy thinking of John's dying words about decoys and how they weren't what they seemed. Could he have been talking about Luke Butler's hand-carved lures that hunters used to attract waterfowl? It was certainly a possibility. Perhaps the pieces of this case's puzzle would fall into place quicker than he thought.

He darted a glance in Betsy's direction, and his fingers tightened around the steering wheel. Her attitude toward him today had shown a big improvement, and he should have been happy. But he wasn't. The way she'd smiled and joked with him had reminded him of a time when he'd looked forward to seeing her every day. However, they weren't the same people they were then. He was a man on a mission, and he couldn't afford to lose sight of why he was here.

Betsy took a bite of her turkey sandwich and glanced at the customers in The Coffee Cup. There were a few unfamiliar faces in the crowd today. Most of them tourists, no doubt. She wiped her mouth on a napkin and leaned toward Mark. "This place is packed today."

He swallowed a bite and picked up his glass of

iced tea. "I always think of that as a sign of a great place to eat."

"It is. I come here quite often at lunch. In fact—"

"Well, would you look who's here, Lizzy? It's that nice, young couple we met at the British Cemetery yesterday."

Betsy looked up into the smiling faces of the retired schoolteachers she had talked to the day before. "Hello, ladies. It's good to see you again."

Mark pushed his chair back and started to rise, but Miranda shook her head. "Don't get up. We were just leaving and saw you sitting here. We wanted to say hello again and thank you for your time yesterday."

"I was glad to share what I know about the cemetery. As I said, it's something we're very proud of here on Ocracoke."

Miranda nodded. "As well you should be." She glanced down at their food and took Lizzy by the arm. "We don't need to interrupt this nice young couple's lunch."

Betsy shook her head. "You're not interrupting anything. I'm glad to see you again."

Miranda smiled. "We really need to be on our way to the General Store. Lizzy dropped her sunglasses this morning and stepped on them before she realized it. She needs to get another pair." She shook her head and wagged a finger at her friend.

"I declare, Lizzy, sometimes I think I was put on this earth just to take care of you."

Lizzy winked at Betsy. "I think it's the other way around. She wouldn't have any idea how to get anywhere if I didn't lead the way."

Miranda laughed and looped her arm through her friend's. "I suppose we take care of each other. We've been doing it for a long time." Miranda pulled Lizzy away from the table. "We hope to see you again before we leave the island."

Mark smiled. "Have a nice day, ladies. I'm sure we'll run into you again before you leave."

"We hope so." Lizzy turned and followed her friend from the restaurant.

Betsy watch the two step out the door then turned back to Mark just as he shoveled several ketchup-covered French fries in his mouth. She grinned, picked up a napkin and reached across the table to wipe at a spot of ketchup in the corner of his mouth. His body stiffened as she dabbed at the spot.

"You always were a messy eater," she said, glancing his way. He stared at her without blinking, and too late she realized what she'd done. She pulled her hand back and dropped the napkin on the table. "I'm sorry, Mark. I shouldn't have done that."

"It's all right," he said, but his voice sounded gruff.

She shook her head. "I guess I got carried away.

I've enjoyed being with you today, and I guess I let myself think the past doesn't matter. But it does."

"Like the night we went to Memphis in May and ate barbecue on the banks of the Mississippi River? And I got sauce all over my face, and you wiped it off with your napkin? I enjoyed that night, Betsy. I don't want to forget the times like that."

She shook her head and pushed back from the table. "I don't want to remember. Maybe in time." She glanced at his plate. "Finish your meal and meet me outside. I'll wait for you on the bench by the front door."

Without waiting for a reply, she headed toward the front door. She'd just put her hand out to open it when he gripped her arm. "You can't leave," he growled. "Wait until I pay, and we'll both get out of here."

"All right." She pulled free and waited as he paid the cashier.

They didn't speak on the way to Mark's car. He opened the door for her and waited until she climbed in. Then he leaned forward. "No matter how you feel about me, don't run off like that again. Okay?"

She jerked her seat belt around her and snapped it in place. "Whatever you say. You're the one in charge."

A long sigh escaped his lips. "Let's skip the

trip to the wood carver's studio today. We'll pick up Treasury's items, then I'll take you back to the bed-and-breakfast."

She nodded, and he closed the door. Betsy clasped her hands in her lap and breathed deeply in hopes of calming her racing heart. She still couldn't believe she'd reached across and wiped Mark's mouth. He was right. For a moment she'd felt just like she did the night they'd sat on the Mississippi River bank and eaten barbecue.

The memory of that night still lingered in the back of her mind, and try as she might she'd never been able to forget. Then she'd thought she was falling in love, but that feeling ended a few days later when she found out the truth about the man she thought she knew.

Now she had to be careful not to get drawn back to the good memories. Mark was the same now as then—an undercover agent who had only one thing on his mind. A friendship with her wasn't part of his plan, and she would do well to keep that in mind.

SEVEN

When Mark stopped the car in the general store parking lot, Betsy jumped out and hurried to the porch. She heard his car door bang shut and knew he was right behind, but she didn't look at him. Instead, she pulled Treasury's list from her pocket and rushed inside.

Mark followed her up one aisle and down another without speaking as she pulled items from the shelf and dropped them in the basket she'd grabbed just inside the front door. She bit her lip and glanced over the list then turned toward the checkout line.

He ambled up beside her and stood with his hands in his pockets as they waited for Sam Isaacs, the owner of the store and the lone cashier today, to check out three customers in front of them. A giggle from behind caught Betsy's attention, and she glanced over her shoulder. Lizzy and Miranda stood in line behind them.

"We meet again," Lizzy gushed.

A smile pulled at Betsy's lips. "So we do. Did you get your sunglasses?"

Lizzy held up a pair and a copy of *Island Life,* the weekly list of island activities. "I did, and I also picked this up. There are several nighttime events we want to attend."

Betsy glanced at the brochure, and a thought popped into her head. "I meant to see if the latest issue of *Newsweek* had arrived." She backed out of the line and turned toward the magazine rack. "Go on in front of me. I'll be back in a minute."

Out of the corner of her eye she saw Mark follow her, but she didn't turn around. They stopped in front of the display, and he reached around her. "Here's a copy."

Before she could reply, a woman's scream pierced the air, and then a man's shout echoed through the store. "Do as I say," he yelled, "and I won't have to hurt this woman."

Betsy and Mark whirled at the same time. A man in a black ski mask stood behind Lizzy and held a gun to her head. A shorter man in a red mask brandished a gun in the direction of the frightened customers at the checkout counter. Sam, who a moment ago had rung up a customer, stood behind the cash register. His face had drained of color, and his dark eyes bulged with fear.

Lizzy's mouth gaped open, and she cast a terrified glance at Miranda, who appeared frozen in place. A tremor of fear surged through Betsy, and she glanced up at Mark. "What can we do to help her?"

"Nothing right now." He put his hand on Betsy's arm. "Do as they say," he whispered.

One of the men glanced their way and motioned toward them. "Hey, you two over there by the magazines, join us."

The basket Betsy held slipped from her hands and tumbled to the floor. Mark put his arm around her waist and guided her toward the men. They stopped a few feet away. "What do you want?" he asked.

The man in the black ski mask tightened his hold on Lizzy and rubbed the barrel of the gun down the side of her face. He nodded to Sam Isaacs. "Open your cash register and empty it into a shopping bag."

Sam's hand shook as he punched a key on the register. The drawer slid open, and he began to pull the money out and stuff it in a bag with the store's logo on the side. The second robber leaned forward. "No checks. Just cash."

When the bag was full, the man in the red ski mask grabbed it from Sam's hand and started to back away. His blue eyes, visible through the slits in the mask, flickered as he scanned the customers. His gaze came to rest on Betsy, and she swallowed the taste of nausea flooding her mouth.

The man eased toward her and pointed the gun at her stomach. His gaze drifted from her face to the necklace she wore. He slipped his fingers beneath the pendant, and Betsy flinched at his touch. Next to her, she felt Mark tense.

"Get away from her." Mark's words hammered in her ear.

The man pulled his hand back, and the pendant bounced against her neck. He turned his attention to Mark and shoved the gun in his face. "Okay, Mister Wiseguy, let's see what you're going to do about it."

Before Betsy realized what had happened, the man grabbed her around the waist, pulled her against him, and stuck the gun to her head. A whimper rolled from her throat as he pulled her backward. She tried to pull free, but he gripped her tighter.

"Please," she whispered. She didn't know if the word was directed to the gunman or Mark.

"Let the old lady go," he called out to his partner. "We'll take Mr. Wiseguy's girlfriend, instead." He waved his gun toward the huddled customers. "If anyone comes after us, I'll kill her."

The other robber shoved Lizzy forward, and Miranda grabbed her before she hit the floor. Both women cast terrified glances at Betsy as the man holding her pulled her toward the door. He glanced over his shoulder before he backed on to the porch. Then he pulled her across the porch and down the stairs. Over her shoulder, she could see the other man who had run past them holding the back door of a car open.

"Put her in here," he yelled to his partner.

She strained against the arm locked around her, but it was no use. There was no way she could break free. "Please," she gasped. "You need to let me go before you get into worse trouble than you already are. There's no way off this island, and the police will find me."

The robber holding her chuckled and dragged her closer to the car's open door. "You think so? Well, your brother will have a hard time doing that."

Cold fear knotted her stomach. How did this man know her brother was a deputy on the island? There could only be one explanation. This wasn't a robbery. These men had come into the store with the intention of abducting her.

The reality of her situation sank in. There was no escape, and from the sound of her kidnapper's voice, he didn't intend for her to be found. What would they do? Kill her? Would she disappear and never be seen again? She shivered with fear. The necklace bounced on her neck again, and Betsy thought of her mother.

Betsy had never known anyone stronger in her faith than her mother. Even when she knew she was dying, her spiritual beliefs never wavered. Now as she faced possible death and what seemed like a hopeless situation, Betsy felt God's love flood her heart. A sudden peace filled her soul. She closed her eyes and breathed a prayer that God would stay with her no matter what happened.

Mark had debated his options from the moment he spun around to see the robbers. Pulling his gun would endanger customers in the store and also lead to questions about why he carried a weapon. It would be better to avoid gunfire, but he wouldn't hesitate if innocent lives were put in danger.

The entire time the robbers were in the store, he'd scanned the shelves and aisles for some kind of weapon, and the display of croquet sets next to the door had caught his attention. The minute the robber disappeared out the door with Betsy, he rushed past Lizzy and Miranda. "Call the police," he yelled over his shoulder to the owner.

He grabbed a croquet mallet in his left hand and one of the wooden balls in his right. Flattening himself against the wall beside the door, he peeked around the door facing and saw the robbers pulling Betsy to a car next to his in the parking lot.

The man in the red ski mask held her around the waist with her arms pinned to her sides and pulled her backward. The other ran ahead to the car and opened the back door. The only way to save Betsy was to stop them before they had a chance to escape with her in the car.

He started to reach for the gun strapped around his ankle but hesitated when two motorcycles roared into the parking lot. The noise from the engines startled the robbers, and they whirled with their guns aimed at the two riders. With Betsy's captors momentarily distracted, Mark bolted through the store's door, took aim with the wooden croquet ball, and hurled it at the man holding Betsy.

The ball sailed through the air and struck the robber between his right shoulder and elbow. His arm jerked, and the gun crashed to the ground. A cry of pain pierced the air as he released Betsy and grabbed his now-dangling broken arm with his left hand.

Gripping the mallet with both hands, Mark leaped down the front steps and charged toward the disabled robber. Betsy scrambled to put some distance between herself and the masked men. Mark swung, and the mallet sank into the man's soft stomach. A groan rumbled in his throat, and he keeled over.

Mark pulled back to swing again just as he heard Betsy's scream. "Mark, look out behind you!"

He tried to turn but it was too late. Something heavy struck his head, and he fell to his knees. He shook his head to clear the ringing in his ears and glanced up in time to see the butt of a gun descending again. He held the mallet with one hand above his head in an effort to deflect the blow and tried to reach his gun, but it was no use. Another pain flashed through his head, and he sprawled facedown on the pavement. Out of the corner of his eye he saw the robber he'd attacked scramble to his feet and jump in the car.

"Mark!" Betsy's cry mingled with the wailing of distant sirens.

"Stand back or I'll shoot!" a voice growled from nearby.

A car door slammed, and an engine roared to life.

Was Betsy safe, or was she a prisoner in the car? He needed his gun, but he couldn't reach it.

Get the gun! Protect Betsy!

Mark flattened his palms against the rough asphalt and tried to push up. It was no use. He tried to call her name, but the only sound that came from his throat was a groan. He sank back to the ground and welcomed the darkness closing in around him.

Mark's eyes blinked open. Where was he? Someone nearby spoke in a soft whisper. He tried to sit up, but strong hands gripped his shoulders and pushed him back down.

"Easy there, mister. You've got quite a bump on the head."

Mark's gaze drifted over the face of the man leaning over him and came to rest on the patch on his sleeve, a six-pointed star with a serpent entwined around a rod in its center. Mark frowned and tried to focus on the emblem. "Th-the Star of Life," he whispered. "Are you an EMT?"

The man chuckled. "That's right. I'm Arnold Culver. I met you yesterday out at Springer's Point."

"W-where am I?" Mark tried to sit up, but Arnold pushed him down again.

"You're lying on a gurney in the parking lot of the Island General Store. Two men tried to hold up the store, and you took on the robbers. I'm afraid you got the worst end of the deal. We're going to transport you to the health center and let Doc check you out."

Mark's heart thudded, and he grabbed Arnold's arm. "Betsy? Where is she?"

"I'm right here, Mark."

He turned his head in the direction of her voice. Tears ran down her face, and she covered his hand with hers. "Are you all right?" he asked.

"I'm fine, thanks to you. But I've been so worried about you." Fresh tears trickled from her eyes.

He rubbed his hands over his eyes and frowned. "I remember charging down the steps toward the car but nothing much after that."

Betsy's hand tightened on his. "I was never so glad to see anybody in my life as I was when you burst out the door. I don't think those guys knew what hit them. You looked like a gladiator swinging that croquet mallet. I heard the bone in that guy's arm break when the croquet ball hit him. Where did you learn to throw like that?"

"I pitched on my college baseball team."

She smiled. "Well, you sure struck that guy out. He even dropped the money in all the excitement. You saved me from being a hostage, and Sam recovered his money, as well."

His head cleared, and what had happened in the store flashed in his mind. He bolted upright on the gurney, and this time Arnold couldn't stop him. "I've got to get after those guys."

This time it was Betsy who grabbed his arm. Her forehead wrinkled with a frown, and she shook her head. "You're not going anywhere but to the health center. Brock and Scott have already been here, taken a statement from everyone, and they put an APB out for the car the robbers were driving. So lie back down and do what Arnold tells you to."

Arnold shook his head and laughed. "I've known Betsy for a long time, and she's a mighty determined woman when she sets her mind to it. I suggest you do what she says."

Mark started to protest, but the glare Betsy directed at him told him it would be best if he didn't. He lay back down. "All right," he grumbled, "but this is a waste of time. I'm fine."

Arnold and his assistant picked up the gurney. As they moved toward the ambulance, Mark's gaze drifted over the crowd gathered in the parking lot. The owner, who he'd seen at the cash register, smiled and waved to him. "Thanks, mister, for saving my money."

Mark smiled and glanced at Lizzy and Miranda. Lizzy had a tissue pressed against her mouth, and Miranda took a step toward the gurney. "I've never seen anything so brave in my life. We're praying you're not hurt badly."

Before Mark could respond, the two EMTs shoved the gurney into the back of the ambulance. Then Arnold climbed in with him and turned to Betsy. "You want to ride with us?"

She shook her head. "No, if you'll get Mark's keys out of his pocket, I'll drive his car and meet you there. I wantto hear what Doc has to say about him."

Mark handed his keys to Arnold, and he tossed them to Betsy. Then the doors closed, and the ambulance began to move. He relaxed and replayed the events in the store in his mind.

He recalled the look of terror on Betsy's face when the man touched the pendant hanging around her neck. Maybe if he'd been quiet instead of telling the robber to leave Betsy alone he wouldn't have decided to use her as a hostage.

Guilt flooded through him at the possibility he had been the reason Betsy was targeted. But the gunmen already had a hostage and the money. Why did they waste time by calling Betsy and him from the magazine shelf and then taunting her? Why didn't they take the money and leave? Betsy's necklace wouldn't have brought much money in a pawn shop. And if they were after money, why didn't they retrieve the dropped bag after he had been knocked unconscious? There were too many unanswered questions. Unless...

Mark's eyes popped open, and an icy fear washed over him. Perhaps robbery wasn't the primary objective for the two. Maybe the men entered the store with another plan in mind and used the robbery to disguise their true purpose— to kidnap Betsy.

The hairs on the back of his neck prickled.

What he feared had come true. Whoever was after Betsy had almost succeeded. If those motorcycles hadn't arrived when they did and distracted her abductors, Betsy might be dead right now.

He had to be more attentive to what was going on around her from now on. He couldn't let his guard down for a minute. It could be the difference in whether she lived or died.

He recognized the number displayed on his cell phone's caller ID right away. He took a deep breath before answering. "Talk to me."

"Uh, there was a problem."

His fingers tightened on the phone. "What do you mean? Do you have her or not?"

"No, you see…"

His fist crashed down on his desk. "What happened?"

"There was this guy with her, and…"

"Did he have a gun?" he demanded.

"N-no."

"But you did. How did he cause a problem against two triggermen who came so highly recommended?"

"It all happened so fast we couldn't do anything. He attacked Vern. Broke his arm. I had to knock the guy out so we could get away. We barely were able to shake the cops."

He ran his hand through his hair and groaned. "This is just great. Where are you now?"

"At the boathouse, but Vern's in a lot of pain. He needs a doctor."

"Well, he can't see one until he gets back to the mainland. Stay in the boathouse until dark. Then I'll send a boat to take you up the coast."

"Thanks." There was a pause. "And I'm sorry about not getting the job done."

He exhaled a deep breath. "Yeah, me too."

He clicked the phone off and glanced across the room to the sofa where his assistant sat. "They didn't get her."

Smoke curled up from the cigarette he held. He stared at the ashes forming on the tip of the cigarette and shook his head. "That's not good news. What do you want me to do?"

He stuck his hands in his pocket, walked to the window and stared outside. Several options were available, but the question remained which would be the best one for the organization. Much as he detested violence, he'd accepted it as a way of life among his new friends on the mainland. They weren't the forgiving kind. They wouldn't hesitate to come after him if he messed up this last shipment.

If he was able to recover the information Betsy had and get the latest merchandise to the mainland, he wouldn't have to worry about them breathing down his neck anymore. His cut would ensure his plan to retire and leave this island. Then he could disappear and live in luxury for the rest of his life.

He took a deep breath and turned back to his assistant. "Pick up those two punks at the boat-house after dark and take them up the coast. Then I want you to get back here and take care of Betsy Michaels."

The man stubbed the cigarette out in an ashtray on a table beside the sofa and stood. "Consider it done."

He watched his assistant walk out the door before he sank down on the sofa. Sometimes he wished he'd never gotten mixed up in the drug trade, but he had to admit it had been lucrative. This last shipment promised to be the biggest they'd ever handled. No way was he going to let Betsy Michaels ruin this for him.

The important thing right now was to retrieve the information John Draper had given her no matter what they had to do. She could have saved herself a lot of trouble if she had done as she was told, but the Michaels girls had always been stubborn. And Betsy was worse than either of her sisters. This time, though, her refusal to give up what she had could prove fatal.

EIGHT

Betsy couldn't sit still another minute. She jumped up from the health center's waiting-room couch and charged across the floor to the desk where the receptionist sat. Mona Davis glanced up from the computer screen she'd been staring at ever since Betsy arrived and smiled.

"Do you need something, Betsy?"

Betsy pointed to the clock over the door that led to the hall where the exam rooms were located. "We've been here forty-five minutes. What's taking Doc so long?"

The pretty receptionist's smile grew larger, and Betsy wondered how often she'd practiced on the friends and family members of patients receiving treatment. "I'm sure he'll talk to you as soon as he knows anything. In the meantime, could I get you something to drink? A soft drink, perhaps? Or a cup of coffee?"

Betsy sank down in a chair beside Mona's desk and sighed. "No, thanks. I'm not trying to be difficult, Mona. It's just that I'm so worried about Mark. He got hurt trying to protect me, and I feel responsible."

The receptionist's eyebrows arched. "No wonder you're worried. I would be the same way if my boyfriend got hurt trying to protect me."

Betsy tried to control the surprise Mona's words produced. Ocracoke Island might host a lot of tourists, but the locals knew all about each other's personal problems. One of the hottest topics on the village grapevine was about the abuse Mona suffered from her boyfriend, Mac Cody. No one could understand why she put up with it.

Betsy's gaze drifted to a vase filled with red roses next to the computer and then to the bruise underneath Mona's left eye. Concern for the young woman she'd grown up with pricked her heart. "Would Mac protect you?"

Mona's forehead furrowed, and she stared at Betsy. "Of course he would. He loves me."

Betsy reached out and grasped Mona's hand. "We've been friends since we were in first grade. I know what a rough time you've had since your parents died and your sister moved away. I don't know why you put up with Mac."

Mona jerked her hand free. "You don't know anything about Mac."

"I know he shouldn't be using you for a punching bag. You deserve better."

Mona's eyes darkened, and she shook her head. "Please, Betsy. My personal life is none of your business."

Betsy searched her mind for words that might offer hope to someone living in an abusive situation. "It's my business because I care about you. A few Sundays ago our pastor spoke about friendship in his sermon. He reminded us that a friend loves at all times, even when bad things happen to us. I've been your friend for a long time, Mona, and that's not going to change. If you ever come to the point you want help, let me know."

A tear trickled down Mona's face, and a sad smile pulled at her lips. "We're not all as fortunate as you are, Betsy. You have a supportive family, and you have a boyfriend who puts himself in danger to protect you."

The word *boyfriend* took Betsy by surprise, and she shook her head. "No, you have it all wrong. Mark isn't my boyfriend. I've known him for a long time, but we're not romantically involved."

Mona tilted her head to one side and let her gaze drift over Betsy's face. "Well, you could have fooled me. From the way the two of you were looking at each other before Doc shooed you out of the exam room, it sure *looked* like there was a lot of chemistry there."

Betsy jumped to her feet and frowned. "No, he's just a friend who's visiting the island."

Before Mona could reply, the phone on her desk rang, and she reached for it. "Ocracoke Health Center. May I help you?"

Betsy turned away and strode to the couch. She glanced at Mona, who was still talking on the phone. The smirk on her face conveyed the message that Betsy needed to deal with her own problems before trying to tell someone else what to do.

Betsy's face burned at the memory of how scared she'd been when her abductors had attacked Mark. She put her palms to her cheeks and wondered if her face betrayed how she felt. She only hoped Mark hadn't gotten the same impression Mona obviously had.

The chime of her cell phone interrupted her thoughts, and she pulled it from her pocket. Scott's number flashed on the caller ID. She jammed the phone to her ear. "Did you catch the creeps who tried to abduct me?"

Her brother's low chuckle vibrated in her ear. "And hello to you, too."

She propped her free hand on her hip and gripped the phone tighter. "I'm sorry, Scott, but this is no time for polite conversation. I want to know what's going on."

"Whoa, Betsy. Are you all right? You don't sound like yourself."

Betsy took a deep breath. There was no need to take out her frustrations on her brother. "I'm sorry. It's not every day I witness a robbery and have a gun held to my head."

"I know, but thanks to Mark you're okay now. And to answer your question, we haven't found the robbers yet, but we did find their car in the parking lot at the lighthouse. No sign of them, though. We talked to the ranger on duty and the tourists there. Nobody remembers seeing anyone near the car." He sighed with frustration. "It's like they vanished into thin air. They've got to be on this island somewhere, but it could be anywhere."

Betsy sank back down on the couch. "Are you going to check the cars at the ferry in case they try to leave the island?"

"We will, but we don't have a description. They wore masks, and the only thing we know is one is nursing a broken arm. That may prove helpful. But Brock and I are on this. We won't give up."

"Thanks, Scott. There's one more thing I think I should tell you. It may be nothing, but it concerns me."

"What is it?"

"When the man was pulling me toward the car, he mentioned my brother wouldn't be able to save me. If I was a random hostage, how did he know my brother was a deputy?"

"This doesn't sound good," he agreed tersely. "I think Mark is right about somebody being after you. What did he say about this?"

"I haven't told him, but I will when I see him again. Doc should be coming out anytime now."

"Tell Mark we'll run by and check on him if we get a chance, but it looks like we'll be tied up for a while."

"That's all right. I'll stay here and see what Doc has to say." The door to the hallway opened, and Doc Hunter motioned for her to follow him. "Here's Doc now, Scott. I'll call you back and let you know what he says."

"Good. And stay close to Mark."

Betsy shoved the cell phone in her pocket and headed down the hallway behind Doc. "How is he?"

He stopped outside the same exam room Betsy had been in the day before and pushed his glasses up on his nose. "He says he's fine, but I'd like to check him out more. I want to airlift him to the mainland and do a CAT scan at the hospital, but he says no. He's determined to go back to Treasury's. Do you think you can convince him to go to the hospital?"

Betsy frowned and shook her head. "I doubt it. He probably thinks he's indestructible. But let me see what I can do."

"I've been arguing with him for thirty minutes and haven't done any good. If you can't convince him, then he's free to go. I'll be in my office. Let me know what he decides."

Betsy pushed the door open and stepped into the room. Mark's long legs dangled over the edge of the exam table, and her heart constricted at the thought of how scared she'd been when he'd been unconscious earlier. "How are you feeling?"

Grinning, he rubbed the back of his neck. "I'll be okay. I've had worse happen to me."

"I suspect you have, but I've never been around to see it happen before." She regarded him through narrowed eyes. "I was scared, Mark."

His gaze didn't waver from her face. "I told you I would protect you."

She shook her head. "I wasn't scared for myself. I knew God would get me through whatever I had to face. It was you I was frightened for. I thought they might have killed you, and I didn't want that to happen."

"It was worth getting hurt if you really were concerned for me." He pushed off the exam table and took a step toward her. His body swayed, and he grabbed the edge of the table to steady himself. Before she had time to think, Betsy wrapped her arm around his waist, and his free hand circled her shoulders as he sagged against her.

Betsy hadn't been this near Mark in a long time, but for a moment time stood still. She closed her eyes and let the familiar feeling of years ago return. She didn't want to remember how she and Mark had laughed together and walked hand-in-hand along the banks of the Mississippi River, but it was no use. Even when she'd proclaimed how much she despised him, she had secretly longed to renew their friendship and see where it would take them. Now he was here, and he had saved her life.

His fingers tightened on her shoulder, and she stared up at him. The muscle in his jaw twitched, and he bent closer. Her breath froze in her throat as his face drew nearer to hers. Then he tensed, and his free hand brushed at her cheek. "You have another smudge on your face."

A chill rippled through her body, and his arm drifted from her shoulders. She swallowed in an effort to suppress the emotions racing through her body and took a step backward to put more distance between them. "You need to listen to Doc and get a CAT scan."

His gaze flitted about the room from one object to another, anyplace but at her. "I don't have time for that. I need to talk to Brock and Scott and see what they've found out."

"I just talked to Scott."

"What did he say?"

As she relayed what Scott had told her on the

phone, Mark rubbed his chin and nodded. He appeared to be in deep thought the longer she talked, but he still hadn't made eye contact with her. When she finished, he took a deep breath. "I need to talk to them. There's something they need to know."

Why wouldn't he look at her? Was he embarrassed because he suspected she thought he was going to kiss her? She couldn't let him know how shaken the encounter had left her. She squared her shoulders and lifted her chin. "Do you want to tell them the real reason the men came into the store was to abduct me?"

His mouth dropped open, and his gaze darted to her face. His dark-eyed stare almost took her breath away. "How did you know?" he demanded.

"The one holding me let it slip. I've already told Scott."

"What did he say?"

"He said they would take care of it. So there's no need for you to talk to them. They can do without your help for a while." He started to interrupt, but she held up her hand to silence him. "So the way I see it is this—you have two choices. You can either go to the hospital or go back to Treasury's where you will have two women fussing over you for the rest of the day." She paused and smiled. "On second thought, you may have four women at your beck and call if Kate and Emma find out what happened."

He let out a long breath, and a slow grin pulled at his lips. "When you put it that way, it's a no-brainer. I'm ready to go to Treasury's house anytime you are." The grin slowly dissolved, and his gaze raked her face. "Besides, I'm not leaving you until I know these guys are in custody."

He moved to step around her, but she reached out and grabbed his arm. "Mark, please don't take your injury lightly. I'll be all right with Brock and Scott."

"No, Betsy," he growled. "I've got a job to do, and I can't do it from a hospital bed in a town miles away from the island." He strode to the door, jerked it open, and turned to face her. "Are you coming with me or not?"

The closeness she'd felt minutes ago shattered, and she clenched her fists at her side. How could she have thought he wanted to kiss her? And what made her think he wanted to stay because he cared for her? To him it was only about the job, and it always would be.

Her nose tingled from struggling to keep tears from flooding her eyes. Ducking her head, she hurried past him and into the hall. She heard him close the door to the exam room and tell Doc he was leaving, but she didn't turn around. She needed time to recover from the hurt his words had inflicted before she faced him. It would never do if he guessed she had let down her guard against him for a few minutes.

She wouldn't do it again.

This morning, Mark had marveled at the beauty of the sunrise over Ocracoke, and now at sunset the sky was just as breathtaking. It reminded him of an artist's giant palette with all the vibrant colors mixed together in sweeping patterns as far as the eye could see. He'd never thought about God much, but if there was a God, He had to be pleased with the picture He'd painted in the sky this afternoon above Ocracoke Island.

Taking another sip of the lemonade Treasury had fixed for him, he stretched out in the wicker chair on the back porch of the bed-and-breakfast and sighed. After all the excitement of the day it was good to sit out here and relax.

For the time being, Betsy was out of danger. She'd been in her studio ever since they got home from the health center. The time away from her had given him the opportunity to reflect on the events of the day.

Brock and Scott had reported an hour ago they still had no leads on the robbers, and that troubled him. At least she was safe here. He would never have suspected she would have been in danger in a crowded store, but she had been.

He rose from the chair and strode to the back-porch railing and grasped one of the posts that supported the roof. The scene from the store flashed into his head, and with it came the fear he'd felt when the men forced Betsy toward their car. Then that thought was replaced by the one at the health center and how close he'd come to kissing her.

How could he have lost control like that? He'd promised himself he wouldn't get emotionally involved again with Betsy. It wasn't fair to her or to him. Then he'd almost blown it.

He closed his eyes for a moment and remembered how she'd looked standing so close to him and how she'd lifted her face to gaze at him. It was almost as if she wanted him to kiss her. Did she? He smacked the railing with his hand.

"No," he muttered.

"No, what?"

He whirled and almost dropped his glass of lemonade at the sight of Betsy. A puzzled expression on her face and a glass of lemonade in her hand, she stood just outside the back door. He walked back to the table and set his glass down.

"I—I was just thinking how I shouldn't have taken you in the store this afternoon. I should have been more careful. I will be in the future."

She pointed to his chair. "You need to sit down

and quit worrying about this afternoon. Everything worked out okay, thanks to you."

He dropped into the chair and waited to respond until she was seated across from him. "I just don't want to fail you again."

She cocked one eyebrow and leaned forward. "What do you mean?"

How could he say what he wanted her to know? He'd practiced it many times through the years, and yet he'd thought he would never have the chance to tell her. Now she sat across from him, and he'd almost kissed her this afternoon. Would she want to know what he'd really felt years ago in Memphis?

He took a deep breath. "I want to explain about Memphis."

The sparkle in her eyes dimmed and was replaced by the wary expression she'd worn at Springer's Point. "There's nothing to explain."

He ignored her reply and nodded. "Yes, there is. I want you to know I never intended to hurt you. I liked you from the moment I came to work at that restaurant. But I have to admit I cultivated your friendship to find out more about Mr. Rousseau." He cleared his throat. "After I got to know you, I realized you knew nothing about what was going on there, but I suspected Brenda—who was one of the waitresses—did."

"I remember Brenda. I never liked her much."

Mark chuckled. "Neither did I. When I told my captain about Brenda, he ordered me to concentrate on her." He paused. "But I couldn't do it. I wanted to be with you, and I knew you wouldn't understand if I suddenly turned my attention to her."

"So what did you do?"

"I kept an eye on her and noticed she went into Mr. Rousseau's office a lot right before she left work. One night after work I hid in the alley where we parked our cars and spotted her and Mr. Rousseau loading bags into the trunk of her car. When she drove away, I saw one of her taillights was out. I called it in, and two police officers stopped her a few blocks from the restaurant." He took a long sip of lemonade and continued. "When they searched her trunk, they found it filled with bags of cocaine. It didn't take long for her to confess. That's the night the police raided the restaurant."

Betsy shook her head. "But if you knew Brenda was involved, why was I taken to headquarters?"

"I tried to tell them you had nothing to do with it, Betsy. My captain chewed me out and told me if I had followed his orders and concentrated on Brenda, we could have raided the restaurant weeks ago. He told me I was too emotionally involved and couldn't make an objective decision and that he was taking me off the case." He clenched his jaw. "When I protested, he told me if I didn't back off, he would see that I never worked another case. He said he was turning the case over to my partner, Bruce Roberts."

Betsy's forehead wrinkled. "I remember him. He's the one who was so nice to me."

"I know. I told him you had nothing to do with it and begged him to get you out of there. He said he would take care of it, and he did."

She regarded him with a steady gaze that made his heart sink. He didn't think she believed him. "Why didn't you tell me all this the night I was taken to headquarters? I begged you to do something, and you just backed away and told me to tell the truth. Then you turned around and walked out. I'd never felt so alone or so betrayed in my life."

He wanted to tell her he remembered how she looked at him and how he'd hated himself for putting her though that, but she wasn't concerned with how he'd felt that night. "My partner was with you, and I knew you were with the person who was going to get you out of there. I did what I was ordered to do and thought I could explain it all later."

Betsy stared at him without moving for a moment. She still had given no indication if she believed him or not. Finally she sighed. "And when you tried to explain, I slammed the door in your face."

"That's right." He winced. "It was the last thing I wanted, but I finally gave up. Then a few months later, I ran into one of your friends, and she told me you'd graduated and left Memphis. She said she thought you were going to New York."

"I was, but once I came home, I knew I couldn't leave the place where I grew up. I began to paint the island waterfowl and landscapes and joined the artisan community here. Will liked my work and let me show it at his gallery. I make a good living by selling my paintings to the tourists, but Will and I also send our work to a gallery in Raleigh. I sell a lot there."

"Which gallery is it?"

"Denning's."

Mark shook his head in disbelief. "I can't believe it. I've been there, but I didn't see anything with your name on it."

She smiled and wagged a finger at him. "Then you're not very observant for an undercover agent."

The sparkle had returned to her eyes, and it gave him hope she had believed his story. He took a deep breath. "Betsy, I hope you believe me. I never meant to hurt you. I agonized over what to do every day. I couldn't tell you what was going on, and I knew we were headed for a showdown I didn't want. I tried to figure a way to get you out of it, but in the end I couldn't."

She smiled, and his heart leaped. "I'm glad you told me, Mark. I've held on to a lot of bad feelings toward you, and I didn't act the way I should have when you tried to explain. Now I think I can move past all that. Can you?"

He nodded. "There's nothing that would please me more."

"You've saved my life twice since you've been here, and I'm glad you've taken this step to heal our friendship." She stuck out her hand. "I hope you'll forgive me for my actions in the past."

He grasped her hand, and his fingers tightened. "I want you to forgive me, too, Betsy. And I promise you while I'm here, I'll do everything in my power to make sure you're protected."

She smiled and pulled her hand free. "I don't doubt that for a moment. You're very good at your job, Mark." She pushed back from the table and stood. "Now why don't we go see what Treasury is cooking for dinner? When I came through the kitchen, I could smell what I thought was her special roast beef. If so, you're in for a treat."

He stood and followed her to the door. Spicy odors filled the air and mingled with the smell of baking bread. His stomach rumbled, but it was the feeling in his heart that thrilled him. He hadn't felt this good in years, and he liked the joy being with her again had brought back to his life.

She walked over to Treasury, who stood at the kitchen sink, and put her arm around the woman's shoulders. Treasury smiled at her, and he recognized the look of love that passed between the two. A memory of his mother smiling at him like that flashed through his mind.

The happiness he'd felt a moment ago evaporated, and he remembered why he had become a DEA agent. Ever since the morning he'd run into the driveway of their home and had seen the bodies of his parents, murdered by a car bomb because of his father's prosecution of the head of a drug ring, he'd known what he had to do.

He'd started on this path years ago, and no matter what he had to give up, he wouldn't budge from his determination. Not until he'd brought to justice every drug dealer he could find. If he had to deny himself a personal life, he would do it. He just had to be careful and not let his feelings for Betsy turn to anything more than the friendship he wanted with her. He'd walked away once, and he could do it again.

He owed his parents that much.

NINE

Even though it had only been one day since a gunman had dragged Betsy across the parking lot at Sam Isaacs's store, it seemed much longer. At Mark's insistence, she'd spent most of the last twenty-four hours in her studio working on her latest painting, but now she was getting restless. Maybe it was the midafternoon sunshine pouring through the big window that had her distracted, but she needed to get outside for some fresh air.

She put the last of her clean brushes and paints away and headed downstairs. As she reached the last step, Mark came through the front door into the hallway. His dark eyes flashed, and his lips curled into a smile. "Are you finished for the day?"

Even though she tried to ignore it, his smile stirred the feelings she'd been experiencing ever since he'd reappeared in her life. "I had to get out of my room. I was about to go crazy in there. I thought I might sit on the back porch for a while."

Something about him was different this afternoon, and it took her a minute to realize what he'd done. "When did you shave your beard?"

He grinned and rubbed his hand over his jaw. "This morning. I thought having it might help me blend in with the crowd at the local hangouts, but it hasn't helped me chase down any leads yet."

"I know you went out last night. Did you not have any luck?"

He shook his head and snorted. "To hear the locals tell it this island is clean. No drugs for sale anywhere."

Betsy sighed. "I wish that were true, but Brock and Scott have arrested several people who had drugs on them or in their vehicles."

"Yeah, that's what they told me." He took a deep breath. "Anyway, I just came by to check on you. Now I'm going over to the wood carver's shop. Did you say his name is Luke Butler?"

"That's right. How about I come with you?"

He tilted his head to one side, and Betsy knew he was considering her suggestion. "I don't know if it's safe for you to be out."

Betsy directed a pleading look at him. "Please take me with you. I've been cooped up in this house all day. I need to get out. And besides, you need me to introduce you to Luke."

He stared at her for a moment before he exhaled and spread his hands in surrender. "Okay, you win. We'll both go."

The words were no sooner out of his mouth than she had the front door open. "Good. Let's get out of here."

He shook his head and grinned. "I think I've just been outsmarted."

"You have. My mother always said she couldn't resist me when I turned on the charm."

His Adam's apple bobbed, and he gazed into her eyes. "I guess I can't, either."

Betsy's breath caught in her throat. Did his words imply he felt an attraction to her? Her denial to Mona at the health center of any romantic involvement with Mark flashed in her mind. In Memphis they'd considered themselves friends, and she was sure that's the way Mark wanted it on Ocracoke, too. She didn't need to start reading something that wasn't there into his words.

"Then what are we waiting for?" She hurried down the front steps and across the yard to his parked car.

Mark's words were still milling around in her mind when he started the car and pulled into the street. The narrow road that curved through the village was crowded with families on bicycles and pedestrians this afternoon, and Mark seemed focused on his driving. Neither of them had spoken.

She pointed to the car's CD player. "Do you mind if I put on some music?"

He shook his head. "I always keep six CDs loaded. Just push one."

She reached out and depressed the button for track one and settled back in the seat. The first notes from a guitar sounded, and she stiffened. She jerked her head around and looked at Mark. "Is that the CD I gave you when I wanted to introduce you to my favorite Christian rock group?"

Gripping the steering wheel tightly, he stared straight ahead. "Yes."

"B-but you told me you didn't like it. You must have been listening to it since it's on your CD player. Why did you keep it all these years?"

He exhaled slowly. "I suppose I kept it because it reminded me of you. I wanted to understand the faith you have and thought I could get an answer from the music you like."

His response stunned her. Although she'd tried many times in the past to tell Mark about God's love for him, he had been vocal about not being a believer. "I assume it made an impression on you or you wouldn't have kept it."

He shrugged. "I'm still listening to it. Still searching for answers."

She studied his profile, but he didn't glance at her. At that moment, Luke Butler's studio came into sight. She pointed to the parking lot beside the small house. "Pull in here."

He stopped the car and started to get out, but she reached out and touched his arm. He stared at her hand a moment before he glanced up. "What is it?"

"I think you know where to look for the answers, Mark. It's just a matter of stepping out on faith."

He bit down on his lip and nodded. "I guess I've never learned to do that."

She sat still and watched him climb from the car. After a moment, she sighed and pushed her door open. Years ago in Memphis, she had prayed for Mark to find peace for whatever had happened in his life. She'd stopped praying for him when she left to come home, and that knowledge made her ashamed. No matter what had happened between them he was still a child of God, and she wanted Mark to know the joy that comes from knowing Him. She would have to see what she could do about helping him accept God's love.

When they entered the studio, Mark looked around in wonder. He'd never seen anything like the displays on tables and shelves across the room. Everywhere he looked he saw carved sculptures of waterfowl—American widgeon, green-winged teal, scoters, ruddy ducks and probably every species of the Outer Banks.

He stopped next to a decoy of a bufflehead and stared at the patch of green above the bird's beak. "The details on these are magnificent."

"Luke is a master wood carver. His decoys are a favorite with the sportsmen who come to the island during hunting season. Of course, I can't stand to think about those beautiful birds being hunted, but a lot of people here make their living by guiding hunters." She smiled. "No matter how many times I come here I'm always amazed at the number of pieces Luke has created since the last time I was here."

Mark glanced around at the people scattered across the studio. "Where is Luke?"

"There he is."

Mark looked in the direction she pointed and saw a man, perhaps in his late sixties, talking to a group of tourists at the back of the shop. He held a decoy of a Northern Pintail and pointed out the markings on the duck's back. He glanced up, spotted Betsy and waved. In a few minutes he excused himself from the group and came toward her. "Betsy, good to see you. Don't tell me you need to buy a decoy?" His gray eyes twinkled behind the wire-rimmed glasses he wore.

"No, I'm not in the market for one today, but my friend may be." She nodded in Mark's direction. "This is Mark Webber, and he's interested in decoys."

Luke turned toward him. "Good. Is there anything I can help you with?"

Mark made a sweeping motion with his hand. "I can't believe what you have in here. Did you do all this yourself?"

Luke chuckled. "I did. I've been carving wood ever since I was a boy and my daddy gave me my first penknife. I carve all kind of wooden sculptures, but decoys are my favorites."

Mark bent over and peered at a sculpture of a snow goose in flight. He started to touch the wing tip but drew his hand back. "Is it all right if I touch it?"

"Sure. Pick it up and get a good look at it."

Mark placed both hands on the piece and held it up to the light. "The workmanship on this is outstanding."

Luke and Betsy exchanged a surprised look. "You sound like you know wood carving," Luke said.

Mark put the piece down, shook his head and backed away. "I've dabbled in it as a hobby since I was a kid, but I can't do anything like this."

"Never can tell until you try." Luke stroked his chin for a moment. "How long you gonna be on the island?"

"A few weeks. Why?"

"I was just thinking," Luke said, "I don't get many folks in here interested in carving. If you want to hang out here with me for a few days, you might pick up some tricks of the trade. You might be interested in seeing the pieces I'm shipping to the mainland this week."

Mark shook his head. "I don't know…" Before he could finish his statement, the bell over the door tinkled. He turned and glanced at the man entering the shop. Dressed in khaki pants, a tucked in T-shirt and a loose, unbuttoned sports shirt, he looked like a typical tourist. But something in the way his eyes darted about the room sent a warning signal. Maybe it was the jagged scar over his left eye that gave him a sinister appearance.

Luke sucked in his breath at the sight of the man. "Excuse me a minute. I need to speak with this customer."

Betsy, who had been examining a carved brant, waved her hand in dismissal. "Don't worry about us. We'll just look around."

Mark watched Luke approach and shake hands with the man. After a few whispered words, Luke called across the room to one of his sales workers. "Take care of the customers. I'll be right back."

The man with the scar glanced over his shoulder at Mark before he followed Luke through a door with an Office sign on the door. Their eyes locked for a moment before the man looked away.

Mark narrowed his eyes and tried to memorize every detail of the man's appearance. He was about to turn back to Betsy when he caught sight of something that jarred him. For a split second the right side of the man's unbuttoned shirt opened to reveal a suspender clip attached to the waist of his pants.

The hair on the back of Mark's neck stood up. Why was a tourist on Ocracoke carrying a gun? And what was he doing in Luke Butler's office? He needed to let Brock and Scott know about this.

Betsy stepped up beside him. "What's the matter?"

He took her by the arm. "We need to leave."

She frowned and tried to pull away. "We just got here. I thought you wanted to talk to Luke some more about his decoys."

"I'll do that tomorrow. I intend to be back here first thing in the morning. There are some questions I'd like to ask Luke."

Betsy relaxed and allowed him to lead her from the studio. Once in the car, he headed toward the bed-and-breakfast. Questions ran through his mind as he drove. Why was the man armed in the middle of vacationing families? What was Luke Butler's connection to him? And could the stranger's appearance in the studio where he had gone have anything to do with the threats on Betsy's life?

He didn't know the answers to those questions, but he intended to keep a close eye on Luke Butler. He had just emerged as a person of interest in John Draper's death and the attacks on Betsy.

Betsy put the last dinner plate in the dishwasher, picked up a dish towel from the kitchen counter and glanced over her shoulder at Kate, who sat at the table with the baby in her arms. "Dinner was delicious, Kate, but you shouldn't have gone to all this trouble."

Kate shook her head and smiled. "It was fun. Being home with the baby has given me a chance to work on my cooking skills. I'm not as good as Treasury yet, but I'm making progress."

"I wish Treasury could have come tonight, but she was tired. She said she wanted to get to bed early."

Lisa entered the kitchen and held up a glass. "I just found this in the living room. I think Emma must have taken it in there."

"That doesn't surprise me," Kate said. "I find dishes all over the house, but it's good to have her here. She's so good with the baby, and he loves her so much." She turned a questioning stare in Betsy's direction. "Scott tells me he took you and

Mark out in the boat yesterday morning. Is everything going all right there?"

Betsy hardly knew how to answer the question. On the surface everything seemed fine, but she couldn't tell her sister and sister-in-law how she was struggling with her attraction to Mark. She sighed. "Yeah, it's fine. I just wish he could wrap up his case and go home."

Lisa dropped down in a chair at the kitchen table and crossed her arms. "Scott said he noticed how Mark watched you during the trip out on the Sound. He thinks Mark might be having thoughts about picking up where the two of you left off in Memphis."

Betsy didn't want to have this conversation. If she didn't understand her feelings about Mark, how could she explain them to anyone else? "Scott's wrong. There was nothing between us before except friendship, and we're trying to regain that. But I'm not sure it's working. I'll just be glad when Mark's gone from Ocracoke and out of my life forever."

Lisa's forehead wrinkled. "But Scott thought…"

Betsy gritted her teeth and tossed the towel she held onto the kitchen counter. "I don't care what Scott said, Mark Webber is the last man in the world I would ever become involved with."

The words had scarcely left her mouth before she sensed a fourth presence in the room. She glanced toward the doorway, and her heart dropped to the pit of her stomach at the sight of Mark standing there. His expression gave no indication whether or not he'd heard her, but she knew he had. How she wished she could take back the words, but she couldn't.

He cleared his throat and stepped into the room. "Scott and Brock have to be up early in the morning. If you're ready, I'll take you back to Treasury's."

She felt numb, but she was able to nod. "I'm ready." She glanced at Kate who started to rise, but Betsy put out a hand to stop her. "Don't get up. We'll show ourselves out. Dinner was delicious. I'll talk to you both tomorrow."

Mark moved aside, but her arm brushed against him as she walked through the door. The contact sent a tingle of pleasure racing up her arm. She clenched her fists and didn't glance at him.

"Thanks for dinner, Kate. I enjoyed it, and I hope we'll get a chance to do this again before I leave the island."

Betsy heard him, but she didn't turn around. She hurried into the living room and hugged Emma, Brock and Scott good-night. Then she fled to Mark's car in the driveway. He followed her but didn't speak as he climbed in.

He started the engine and reached over and punched the CD player before he pulled out into the street. They rode back to the bed-and-break-fast with the music of her favorite Christian rock group filling the silence between them.

The closeness she had felt to Mark earlier in the day seemed to have disappeared. She wished she could bring it back, but she didn't know how. When they entered Treasury's house, he walked her to her studio door and waited for her to enter. She turned to face him.

"Mark, I'm sorry if you heard what I said to Kate and Lisa. I didn't say it to hurt you."

He nodded. "I know. You only said what we both know is the truth, Betsy. There's nothing between us, and there never will be."

Hearing the words he spoke cut through her heart like a knife, but she tried to smile. "We're still friends. Right?"

A sad smile pulled at his lips. "We're still friends. Sleep well, Betsy. I'll see you in the morning."

She watched him walk back to his room and wondered if the slump in his shoulders was caused by what she'd said. She shook her head. No, he was probably tired. She stepped inside her room and closed the door behind her.

The moment the door closed an uneasy feeling rushed through Betsy's body. She'd left the lamp on the bedside table burning earlier, but the room was now in total darkness. She felt for the light switch on the wall and flipped it, but nothing happened. The hallway lights had been burning when she came upstairs, but her room could be on another circuit breaker. She'd better go to the electrical box in the utility room and check it out.

A soft breeze blew across the room, and Betsy froze. In the moonlight she could make out the fluttering curtains. She hadn't left the window open. She remembered checking it before she left.

Betsy fumbled for the door knob, but before she could pull it open, a figure materialized from the darkness and forced himself between her and the door. Strong fingers circled her neck, and the barrel of a pistol rammed against her temple. "If you make a sound, I'll kill you and then kill your boyfriend when he comes to your rescue. Do you understand?"

Betsy twisted in an attempt to break free, but the fingers tightened. "Yes," she squeaked.

"Good." He pushed her backward across the room until she bumped up against her desk. Her hands dangled at her side, but his body pinned her against the desk. "Now, where is it?" he hissed.

Tears welled in her eyes, and she tried to shake her head. "I—I d-don't know what you're talking about."

He pressed the gun harder against her head. "I'll kill you if you don't tell me."

What did he want? "I—I d-don't have anything."

Betsy felt his body tense, and she closed her eyes. Was he getting ready to squeeze the trigger? He pushed her again until she was bent back over the desk. Frantic now at her impending death, she stretched her arms behind her and clawed at the desk's surface in search of a weapon. Anything to help her. Her fingers brushed the Degas mug with its assortment of pens and pencils inside. *And a pair of scissors for trimming excess canvas.*

She grappled for the mug, and her fingers skimmed over the contents until she felt the scissors. Wrapping her fingers around the handle, she slipped the scissors out of the mug and held them at her back.

"I'm tired of playing games. I'll give you one more chance. Now tell me where it is."

"I've told you I don't know." Her voice broke on the last word.

He glanced over his shoulder toward the bed. "All right, you asked for it. A pillow ought to muffle the gunshot sound. Then I'll tear this room apart until I get what I came after."

Her eyes had now grown accustomed to the dark, and she could make out his figure. Dressed in black, he blended in well in the darkened room. Out of the corner of her eye, she could also make out the shape of the gun he held. He pulled the gun a few inches away from her head and yanked her forward.

As she stumbled toward him, she swung her hand around and buried the scissors in the soft flesh of his stomach. She couldn't see the expression on his face, but she heard his groan. The hand holding the pistol dropped away from her head, and she pulled the scissors out and rammed them in again.

"Mark!" she screamed at the top of her lungs. "Mark! Help me!"

The man clutched at his stomach and staggered backward. Betsy tried to run past him, but he grabbed her by the arm and spun her back. "I'm not done with you yet," he muttered.

The door crashed open, and light from the hall flooded into the room. It illuminated the figure standing in front of her, and recognition kicked in. She'd seen this man in Luke Butler's studio. She remembered because of the scar over his eye.

"Let her go, or I'll shoot!" Mark's voice from the doorway bounced off the walls.

Betsy's heart leaped at the sight of Mark, his legs spread in a wide stance and both hands clutching the pistol aimed at the man. Her attacker whirled, faced Mark and raised his gun. Before he could fire, the report of Mark's gun split the air, and the man slammed back against the desk. The gun dropped from his hand, and Betsy scooped it up.

A look of disbelief flashed across the man's

face, and he stared at the bloodstains spreading on his pants and shirt. He touched the spot where she'd first stabbed him and glared at her. With a roar, he pushed away from the desk and ran toward the window.

"Stop!" Mark yelled.

Mark raised the gun again, but before he could fire, the man jumped through the open window. A loud thud signaled his impact with the ground two floors below. Mark rushed over and peered out the window. Betsy tried to move, but her legs refused to cooperate. "Do you see him?" she asked.

Mark turned and nodded. "He's on the ground in the yard. I'll go check on him. You call 911."

Betsy pulled her cell phone from her pocket, but her fingers shook so violently that she thought she might not be able to punch in the numbers. She'd just finished speaking with the 911 dispatcher when Treasury hobbled into the room. Panting for breath, she hurried toward Betsy and held her at arm's length.

"Are you all right? I've never been so frightened in my life."

Betsy wiped at the tears on her cheeks and tried to smile. "I'm all right."

"What on earth happened up here? The guests are all huddled in the hall scared to death."

Treasury's mouth dropped open as Betsy related

the events of the past few minutes. "But thanks to Mark I'm all right now," she said as she finished.

Treasury wrapped her arms around Betsy and hugged her. "Thank goodness. I don't know what I'd do if anything happened to you."

Mark walked back into the room at that moment and stopped beside her. "Brock and Scott are already here. They're in the backyard, but they'll be up in a minute to check on you. We searched the man's clothing, but he didn't have any identification on him. I recognized him, though. He was at Luke's studio."

Betsy nodded. "I know. Is he alive?"

Mark exhaled sharply. "No. And that means we can't question him about who sent him here and what he wanted."

The sinister tone of the man's voice flashed in Betsy's mind, and she began to shake. The tears she thought had stopped returned full force. "He was going to kill me, Mark. He pushed me back toward the bed to get a pillow to muffle the sound. He would have killed me if…"

Her body began to shake with the sobs that erupted from deep within her soul. Mark reached out and gathered her into his arms. He pulled her close and held her so tightly she could feel the beat of his heart. "It's all right, Betsy. I'm here, and I'll stay with you."

She buried her head against his chest and

wrapped her arms around him. It seemed so right to be in Mark's arms. She couldn't deny it anymore. This is where she'd wanted to be since she'd first met him in Memphis. But her feelings didn't make any difference. Mark didn't want a relationship, and she would have to make sure he never guessed how she felt.

TEN

Betsy didn't know if she would ever be warm again. Even four hours after the attack in her studio, her body still shivered at what she had experienced. A hand squeezed her shoulder, and she glanced up from where she sat at Treasury's kitchen table into the face of her brother. He poured her another cup of coffee and eased into a chair across from her. Mark and Brock sat on either side of her.

She picked up the coffee and tried to bring the cup to her mouth, but her hand trembled so she had to set it down again. Tears filled her eyes, and she bit down on her lip. Brock covered her hand with his. "I talked to Kate. She's beside herself because she can't be here, but the baby and Emma are both asleep. She wants me to bring you to our house."

"That's a good idea, Betsy," Mark said. "Your studio is a crime scene now, and you can't go back in. I can take you to Kate's house if you want me to."

"Maybe later." She clasped her hands in her lap and rocked back and forth. She could almost feel those cold fingers still around her neck. "I didn't see him in the dark. Why didn't the light come on?"

"He'd unscrewed the lightbulbs," Mark said. "He wanted to take you by surprise."

"I was so scared." She stared at Mark and remembered how it had felt to be in his arms. A tear slipped from her eye. "I killed a man, Mark."

He sprang from his chair, knelt beside her and grabbed her by the shoulders. His fingers tightened their hold, and Betsy almost gasped at the blazing rage in his eyes. "The fall from the window killed him, Betsy. Not the gunshot wound in his shoulder, and not you. But he came here to murder you, and you had every right to protect yourself. I won't have you feeling guilty for something that wasn't your fault. Do you understand?"

"Mark's right, Betsy. You can't blame yourself for what happened," Brock said.

She glanced across the table to Scott, and he nodded. "They're right. When you have time to think about this, you'll realize what we're saying is true."

Betsy heard the comforting words coming from her brother and her brother-in-law, but it was the burning concern she saw in Mark's eyes that made her want to believe them. She tried to smile at him. "This is three times you've come to my rescue. How can I ever repay you?"

He released her and moved back into his chair. "By helping us catch these guys. Brock and Scott are going to question Luke in the morning to see what connection he has to the dead man, but there's some reason they keep coming after you. They are convinced John said something or gave you something before he died. Are you sure you haven't forgotten something?"

She shook her head and clasped her hands in front of her on the table. "I've already told you everything he said."

"About the decoys?"

"Yes. All he said was to tell him the decoys aren't what they seem."

Mark reached across the table, covered her hands with his, and leaned closer. "There has to be something else. Think, Betsy. Was there anything at all out of the ordinary that he said or did?"

Her brow wrinkled, and she searched her mind for something she might have overlooked. It was as if her mind was on rewind, and she concentrated on everything that happened from the time John Draper stumbled out of the woods. There had to be something. But what was it?

After a moment, she began to speak her thoughts. "He came toward me, and I helped him ease down to the ground. I took my phone out of fanny pack and told him I was going to call the police. That's when he said they caught him. I thought he meant someone had followed him and looked over my shoulder. I remember I felt his hand fumbling at my fanny pack, and I turned back to him. Then I…"

She stopped and took a deep breath. Mark squeezed her hands, and she turned to stare at him. "Then what?" he urged.

Her heart pounded like a bass drum, and she jumped to her feet. "I'd forgotten about my fanny pack!" Mark, Scott and Brock shot to their feet, too. She turned to Mark. "That night when I emptied my fanny pack there was a pen in it I didn't remember putting in there."

Mark cast a quick glance in Brock's direction and then back to her. "Where is it now?"

"In the Degas mug. I'll get it."

She started to leave, but Mark shook his head. "You don't need to go back in there. I'll get it for you."

Before she could respond, Mark had dashed from the kitchen. Scott and Brock both had puzzled expressions on their faces. "Was there anything unusual about this pen?" Scott asked.

She dropped down into her chair and shook her

head. "It was just a black pen like they have on the desk at the bank with the deposit slips. I thought I had probably picked it up there."

Brock and Scott settled back into their chairs, but their expressions told her they thought this might be the lead they had been looking for. Within minutes, Mark hurried into the room with the mug in his hand, set it in front of Betsy and took his seat. "Which one is it?"

Betsy's body stiffened at the sight of the mug. The memory of how she had grappled to find the scissors filled her with a paralyzing fear. Her attacker's agonizing groan as the blades plunged into his body still rang in her mind, and she didn't know if she would ever be able to forget how she had fought for her life.

Mark reached out and grasped her hand. "Betsy, show us which one it is." His voice had a soothing effect on her, and she took a deep breath.

She lifted her hand and pulled the black pen from the jumbled collection in her pencil holder. "This is it." She held it out to Mark.

He took the pen from her and examined it on all sides. "It looks like an ordinary ballpoint pen."

Brock frowned and leaned over to get a better look. "Do you think he might have written some message and hidden it in the barrel of the pen?"

Mark shrugged. "Could be. I'll take it apart."

He grabbed the cap of the pen and tugged it off.

Mark's eyes widened, and all four of them gasped at the same time. Betsy couldn't believe what she saw. It was more than a pen.

Mark shook his head, chuckled and held it out for them to see. "Would you look at that? The other end of the pen is a USB flash drive. John must have downloaded some information on it."

"That's what he meant!" Betsy slapped her palms down on the table. "He said they caught me. I thought someone was after him, but he must have meant they found him downloading something they didn't want anyone to know."

Mark held the flash drive up in front of his face and peered at it. "It must be important information because they killed him for it and wanted to kill Betsy to get it back." He jumped to his feet. "Treasury has a computer in her office. Let's see what's on here."

Mark hurried from the kitchen with Brock and Scott close behind, but Betsy couldn't move. A ballpoint pen with a flash drive on the other end placed in her fanny pack by a dying man. That's what had made her the target of killers. And tonight the man in her room had almost succeeded.

She folded her arms in front of her on the table and laid her head on them. For the past few days, her life had been like a bad dream. Tonight it had turned into a nightmare. She no longer doubted her life was in danger. That illusion had died the minute icy fingers clamped around her throat.

The man who had attacked her was dead, but whoever had hired him was still on Ocracoke Island. When they found out the hit man they sent to kill her was dead instead, she would be in more danger than ever before. She wouldn't be safe until everyone associated with her assailant was caught and put in jail.

Mark could hardly contain his excitement over the discovery of the flash drive. John had given his life to obtain whatever information was on it, so it had to be something important. With Scott and Brock right behind, he rushed into Treasury's office and headed to her computer. The screen came to life the moment his fingers touched the keyboard. He inserted the flash drive in the USB port and was about to open it when he glanced around and noticed Betsy hadn't followed them into the room.

Scott and Brock crowded behind him and peered over his shoulder. Brock jabbed him in the shoulder. "This could be what we've been waiting for."

Mark frowned and stared at the door. "Where's Betsy?"

"She's probably still in the kitchen. Go on and open it. Let's see what's on it."

Mark's fingers touched the keyboard, but a sudden thought stopped him. Not only had John died for this flash drive, but it had also been the cause of the attempts on Betsy's life. Maybe she didn't want to see what was on it, and maybe the attack tonight had affected her more profoundly than any of them knew.

She had fought for her life tonight more than he'd ever seen anybody do in all his years of police work. Even though she'd survived, he suspected the ordeal had wounded her in a way only she could see—in her spirit. No matter what he'd said to try and ease her guilt, she knew she contributed to a man's death, and she was suffering because of it.

Mark glanced back at the keyboard and then toward the door. Betsy still hadn't appeared, and he grimaced. Scott nudged him in the back. "What's the matter? Aren't you going to open it?"

Why was he hesitating? The answer popped into his head. For the first time in years, something else mattered to him besides the case he was working on. The truth he'd refused to recognize couldn't be withheld any longer. His feelings for Betsy were the most important thing in his life. Now she sat alone in the kitchen, and she needed someone.

He pushed back from the computer and stood.

"I'm going to check on Betsy. You guys see what you can find on the flash drive."

Without waiting for Scott and Brock to question him, he strode from the room. He balled his fists at his sides and shook his head in resignation. Facing the truth about loving Betsy should have made him happy, but it didn't. Not after overhearing her tell Kate and Lisa he was the last person in the world she would ever become involved with. But it was probably for the best she felt that way. There was no way an undercover cop could have a normal life with a wife and family.

He stopped at the kitchen entrance and propped his hand against the doorjamb. Betsy still sat at the table with her head resting on her arms. He didn't think she was crying, but her drooping shoulders told him he'd been right about her wounded spirit.

"Betsy," he murmured, "are you all right?"

She jerked her head up and shot a wild-eyed stare at him. "What are you doing back? Have you already opened the flash drive?"

"No…Scott and Brock are looking at it. I wanted to come back and see about you. How are you feeling?"

She wiped at a tear in the corner of her eye, and he had to force himself not to rush over to her and wrap his arms around her. Instead he walked to the table and eased into the chair next to her. "I can still feel those fingers on my throat and hear how he groaned when I stabbed him with the scissors. I don't think I'll ever forget what happened tonight."

He slid his hand across the table and wrapped his fingers around hers. "You may never totally forget, but it will get better in time."

Her fingers tightened on his, and she glanced down at their hands locked together. "I've been thinking about the attempts on my life. I think I may be in more danger than ever now that the drug dealers' hit man is dead. What am I going to do, Mark?"

"I won't let you out of my sight until these guys are caught."

"And what if you don't catch them? You can't stay on Ocracoke forever. You'll have to leave sometime."

One tear slid down her cheek, and the sight of it set his mind reeling. He longed to tell her he would stay forever if need be, but he knew he couldn't. "Scott and Brock are here for you, too."

"I know, and I'm grateful for them. Right now I feel frightened and kind of lost. I can't get in my studio, and I'm afraid to go home. I wish I could get off the island for a few days. Maybe that would give me time to come to grips with what's happened."

"I think…"

Footsteps at the door interrupted him, and he glanced around to see Brock and Scott entering the kitchen. Both of them frowned. Brock held out the flash drive. "Bad news, Mark. We opened this up and scrolled through the documents. They appear to be some kind of ledger sheets, but they're in code. We have no idea what they say."

Mark pounded his fist on the table and pushed to his feet. "I can't believe this. We have what they want, and we can't read it."

He strode across the kitchen to the sink and grasped the edge of the counter on either side with his hands. Betsy was right. She was in more danger now than ever, and he had promised to stay with her. But this new development needed immediate attention. He had to get the flash drive to Raleigh and let their lab people take a crack at breaking the code. How could he do both?

An idea popped into his head, and he let out a long breath of air. He turned to face Brock and Scott. "I need to get this flash drive to Raleigh right away. I'm going to call my superior and have him send a helicopter for me. I want to get this thing off the island before something happens and the smugglers recover it."

Brock nodded. "Good idea."

He glanced at Betsy, whose mouth had drawn

into a grim line. Mark took a deep breath. "And I want to take Betsy with me."

Betsy arched an eyebrow. "You want me to go with you?"

"Yes." He returned to the table and slid into the chair next to her. "You're in danger here, Betsy. Brock and Scott can't be with you every minute. They have a job to do. I live with my sister in Raleigh, and there's an extra bedroom. You can stay with us for a few days while I'm at headquarters."

She frowned and glanced at Scott, who nodded. "I think that's a good idea, Betsy. It'll do you good."

Mark leaned closer to her. "You said you wished you could get off the island for a few days. This may be what you need. You can rest and try to sort out everything that's happened to you. Then when we get back, your studio will be ready, and you can move back in."

She said silent for a moment and appeared to be debating his invitation. "You're sure your sister won't mind?"

"Of course not. She'll love having you there. What do you say?"

A smile lit her face. "I say I'd like to go to Raleigh with you."

His heart pounded, but he managed to keep his emotions in check. "It's 2:00 a.m. now. I'll call headquarters and tell them to get a helicopter on the way. We'll go by your house and pick up some clothes on our way out to the airfield." He gave a curt nod. "If all goes well, we should be able to have breakfast in Raleigh."

Scott took her by the arm and helped her to her feet. "You can wait in the hallway outside your room while I get anything you need to take with you."

"I appreciate that, Scott."

He put his arm around her shoulders and hugged her. "What are big brothers for? Now come on and let's get you ready for your trip."

Mark watched as Scott and Brock left the kitchen with Betsy. He could hardly believe that Betsy had agreed to go home with him, and it thrilled him. He would have the opportunity to give her a glimpse into his life. She would meet his sister and see where he worked.

When he had known Betsy in Memphis, he had never talked about his personal life, and she knew very little about him. He was glad she was going to get to know what had made him the person he had become. But mainly he wanted to keep her safe, and he intended to do everything he could to see that she remained alive and well. He just hoped the smugglers didn't get wind of Betsy's whereabouts. She needed some time to recover from all she'd been through, and he intended to make sure that happened.

He rolled over, glanced at the clock on the bedside table and reached for his ringing cell phone. It had to be important for somebody to be calling at three in the morning.

"Hello," he growled.

"We have a problem."

He sat up in bed and frowned. "What?"

"Clive's dead."

"Dead?" he bellowed and jumped from the bed. "How did that happen?"

"I don't know yet. I was waiting on the next street for him when I heard sirens. I got as close as I could to the house without being seen. Brock Gentry and Scott Michaels were in the backyard at Treasury's with that guy that's been hanging around with Betsy. I could see Clive's body on the ground, and I hightailed it out of there."

He pounded his fist against the wall and cursed under his breath. "Anything else I need to know?"

"Yeah… I went back to the Blue Pelican and stayed for a while. Then I drove back by the bed-and-breakfast. Betsy and her friend were just leaving. I followed them to her house. Then they went to the airstrip. They got on a helicopter and took off for the mainland."

"This isn't good. If she's gone, that means she

probably has the flash drive with her." He paced for a moment before he stopped. "Okay, there's nothing we can do now. We need to concentrate on getting that new shipment out of here. Until then, make sure your informant keeps us up-to-date on anything dealing with Betsy."

"Right, boss."

"Betsy has to come home sometime. And when she does, we'll be waiting for her. She'll wish she'd given me that flash drive the first time I asked. The next time I won't be so nice."

He disconnected the call and walked to the window. Darkness still covered Ocracoke, but he doubted he could go back to sleep. Thoughts of his partners on the mainland and what they would do when they found out he had allowed a DEA agent to steal all their records troubled him. There was only one thing to do. Get the last shipment to the mainland and get away from this island. He had enough money to disappear and live quietly for the rest of his life.

There was still the question of Betsy. He sank down in a chair, propped his elbows on the arms and tented his fingers. He tapped them together while he tried to decide how he was going to repay her for all the trouble she'd caused him.

Within an hour of making the decision to go to Raleigh, Betsy and Mark boarded the helicopter used for emergencies on the island and flew to the mainland. From there, another helicopter sent by Mark's superior picked them up and transported them to Raleigh.

At the Raleigh field office of the DEA, Mark left her in the break room and disappeared into his superior's office. An hour later she felt as if she was fading fast. Even two cups of coffee hadn't helped.

She raised her hand to her mouth in an attempt to stifle a yawn just as Mark walked into the room. The man who Betsy had caught a glimpse of in the hallway earlier entered behind him. She pushed to her feet and stood beside Mark.

"Betsy, I'd like you to meet William Fowler. He's the head of this field office."

He smiled and held out his hand. "I'm happy to meet you, Ms. Michaels. Mark has told me what an ordeal you've had for the past few days. I want you to know our office will do everything we can to find the people who have terrorized you."

Betsy placed her hand in his. "Thank you, Mr. Fowler. Mark has gone beyond the call of duty in protecting me. I really appreciate it."

Mr. Fowler nodded his agreement. "Mark is one of our top agents. He never gives up until he's closed a case, and I know he won't give up on this one, either. Of course, Agent Draper's death was a tragedy for us, but I'm glad you were able to give us the information he died protecting."

"From what I understand, the contents of the flash drive were in some kind of code. I hope your experts can figure it out."

"I'm sure they will." He glanced at his watch and then at Mark. "Since you've both been up all night, go get something to eat and get some rest. As soon as we know anything, I'll let you know."

Mark rubbed the back of his neck and wiggled his shoulders. "I know Betsy is tired, but I'll stay if you need me."

Mr. Fowler shook his head. "No. You go on home, and I'll call you if we find out anything." He smiled at Betsy. "It was nice meeting you. I hope we can catch these guys so you will feel safe again."

"Me, too," she said. "And thank you again."

Betsy reached for her purse hanging on the back of her chair, looped it over her shoulder, and turned back to Mark. His tired eyes glanced at the clock on the wall. "I called my sister when we got to Raleigh. She's a nurse and worked the night shift at the hospital, so she should be getting off work in about an hour. I told her we'd meet her at home. I may have time to fix breakfast for all of us before she gets there."

"You're going to cook?" Betsy couldn't control the laugh rumbling in her throat.

"Why is that so funny?"

She shook her head and laughed again. "A big strong man who chases drug dealers for a living? I can't believe you'd even know your way around a kitchen."

He laughed and took her by the arm. "Come with me, and I'll introduce you to my culinary skills. I guarantee you've never tasted anything like my cooking."

"That's what I'm afraid of." She glanced up at him, and her heart raced.

What had happened to her in the last few days? A week ago, she couldn't even think of Mark without getting angry. Now she looked forward to every minute they spent together. She knew the time would come when he would leave, but she didn't want to think about that now.

All she wanted was to enjoy being with him. When he did leave, she would be left with good memories, not those like she had carried from Memphis. She just hoped in the future when she recalled the good times it would be enough to soothe her heartache at not having him in her life.

ELEVEN

Betsy almost had to pinch herself to believe she sat at the kitchen table in Mark's house and watched him bustle about like a master chef. Her stomach growled at the aroma of frying bacon and perking coffee. She pressed her hands against her abdomen and sighed.

"I don't know when I've ever been so hungry. Everything smells so good."

He flipped a pancake in the pan on the stove, grabbed the coffee pot and poured her another cup of coffee. "Give me a few more minutes and we'll be ready." He glanced at the clock on the wall above the refrigerator. "Laura ought to be here any minute."

She took a sip and set the cup back in its saucer. "Laura? I don't think you've ever told me your sister's name. In fact, I don't think you ever mentioned having a sister before."

He turned from the stove with a platter of pancakes and set it on the table. The muscle in his jaw twitched, and he reached back for the dish containing the bacon. He didn't speak until he'd set the food on the table and slid into his chair. "I'm sorry, Betsy."

"Sorry for what?"

He took a deep breath and stared into her eyes. "With the kind of job I have, it's a good idea to keep your private life out of the picture. The people I investigate wouldn't hesitate to hurt Laura if they thought they could get to me. That's why I don't talk about her."

Betsy leaned back in her chair and tried not to let her expression convey her puzzlement. Truth was, Mark baffled her. He'd demonstrated his bravery in the past few days, and at times she'd sensed he might care about her. But Mark's thoughts and feelings still remained a mystery to her.

After a moment, she forced a smile to her face and sat up. "Now that I think about it, I used to rattle on and on about my family when we were in Memphis, and you never mentioned yours. I assumed you didn't have any."

He nodded. "I should have told you, but I guess old habits are hard to break."

The back door suddenly opened, and a woman's voice rang out. "Anybody home?"

Mark sprang from his chair, dashed across the room, and threw his arms around his sister. Betsy tried to get a look at her, but Mark's body blocked her view. "Laura, I'm so glad to see you," he said.

"It's good to have you home. Now where's your friend?"

He stepped to her side but kept his arm around her shoulders. Betsy's gaze raked the willowy brunette dressed in green scrubs. With their dark hair and eyes, anyone could see the family resemblance. Mark glanced down at his sister, and his eyes beamed with love. "Betsy, this is my sister, Laura."

Smiling, Laura stepped forward with her hand extended. "It's so good to meet you, Betsy. Mark has told me so much about you."

Betsy pushed to her feet and took Laura's hand. "I hope it's all been good. Although I'm afraid I've been quite a bother to him for the past few days. He's had to spend his time protecting me. In fact, he's saved my life three times."

A startled expression crossed Laura's face. "He didn't tell me that."

Mark shook his head and motioned to the food on the table. "It was nothing. Now go get washed up and come eat your breakfast. I've cooked all this food, and I don't want it to get cold."

"Aye, aye, sir." Laura clicked her heels together, gave him a salute and winked at Betsy. "I'll be back in a minute."

He waved his hands at her to shoo her from the

kitchen. "I'll pour you a cup of coffee while we wait for you."

By the time Mark had set the coffee at Laura's place she reentered the room and dropped into her chair. She inhaled deeply and smiled. "This looks so good. Mark inherited our mother's cooking skills, but I'm afraid I didn't. I can hardly wait for him to come home so I can have a decent meal."

"I'm learning all kinds of things about Mark I didn't know." Betsy cast a glance at him, but he looked away.

"He's a wonderful brother," Laura said, and then clasped her hands in her lap. "But before we eat, I would like to say grace. Do you mind, Betsy?"

"Not at all. We say grace at every meal at home."

Mark quirked a brow. "When did you start praying, Laura?"

She took a deep breath and straightened her shoulders. "I've been going to church with a friend for the last few months, and I've turned my life over to God. I pray all the time now. I'm glad you're home so I can tell you about it."

Betsy reached out and squeezed Laura's arm. "That's wonderful. My faith is very important to me. I don't know how anybody gets through a day without knowing God is with them."

Laura gave a slight nod and looked toward her

brother. "I don't, either. Now if you'll bow your heads, I'll say grace."

"All right," Mark mumbled.

They bowed their heads and Laura began to pray. "Dear God, thank You for this day and the food You've set before us. Thank You for bringing my brother home safely again. I pray You will continue to protect him and guard his steps. And thank You, Lord, for our new friend Betsy and for saving her life. I pray we can all be a blessing to each other. Amen."

Betsy opened her eyes and glanced around the table. A smile curled Laura's lips as she picked up the platter of pancakes and speared two of them. Mark didn't make eye contact with either of them and seemed to be in a world of his own. She wondered what he was thinking and how the news of Laura's newfound faith had affected him.

Her stomach growled again, and she laughed. "I'd forgotten how hungry I am." She took the platter from Laura and slid two pancakes onto her plate before passing it to Mark. "Now let's see if Mark is as good a cook as you say."

Thirty minutes later, Betsy knew Laura hadn't exaggerated about Mark's cooking. She'd never felt so stuffed and content. Now, as she drained her coffee cup, exhaustion began to seep through her body. Laura, on the other hand, looked as if she was ready to run a 5K race.

Laura pushed back from the table, stood and stretched. "You've both been up all night, and I know you're tired. I'll show Betsy to her room, and then I'll do the dishes."

Mark shook his head and reached for their plates. "No, I'm okay. You've been working all night at the hospital. I'll clean up here while you show Betsy to the guest room. I need to check in with headquarters before I get a few hours of sleep."

Betsy picked up her plate and handed it to him. "Breakfast was great, Mark, and thank you for all you've done for me this past week."

He took the plate from her and smiled. "No need to thank me. I was just doing my job."

"I know," she said, then followed Laura out of the kitchen and down a hallway.

Mark's sister pointed to a room at the end of the hall. "I'm going to put you in my room while you're here because it has a private bathroom. I'll take the spare room."

"No," Betsy protested, "I don't want you to do that."

"I insist. When we moved into this house, Mark made me take the master bedroom because it had a bathroom." She pointed to a room on her left. "This is where he sleeps when he's here, which isn't very often."

Betsy glanced through the open door into the

bedroom and halted. A bed sat against one wall, and two glass-front cabinets containing the most beautifully carved figures she'd ever seen sat against another. Other carvings covered a desk and a small dresser. She turned to Laura, who had stopped beside her. "Did Mark do all those?"

"Yes. They're good, aren't they? He has quite a talent. In fact, he wanted to go to an art school and study, but he chose a college that offered a criminal justice degree, instead."

"With such talent, why would he do that?"

Laura's chin trembled. "Has Mark ever told you about our parents?"

"No. To be honest, I didn't know about you until last night."

A sad look drifted into Laura's eyes. "That doesn't surprise me. He doesn't talk about his family to anyone. Did you know we grew up in Memphis?"

Betsy shook her head. "Not really. I guess I assumed he did because that's where I first met him."

"Our father was a federal prosecutor. When Mark was twelve and I was ten, our father was involved in prosecuting the head of a drug ring. One morning when he was leaving for work, my mother went with him because her car was in the shop. It was summertime, and Mark and I were still eating the breakfast our housekeeper had fixed when we heard an explosion." She released a long, shuddering breath. "A car bomb killed both of them in our driveway. Mark and I ran outside, and he went wild trying to get to them, but it was no use. Our housekeeper had to hold him to keep him away from the fire."

Betsy's heart thudded at the thought of what it must have been like for a young boy to see his parents die that way. "How horrible."

"Yes, it was. After the funeral we were sent to live with an aunt and uncle, but Mark has never recovered from their deaths. He decided the only way he could honor them was to become a law enforcement officer and try to get every drug dealer he could off the streets. That's what he's dedicated himself to doing, and he's pushed everything else out of his life. That's why I'm so thankful for the few times a year he comes home."

"I understand," Betsy said softly.

"But," Laura hesitated as if she chose her words carefully, "I sense something different about Mark's relationship with you, Betsy."

"What do you mean?"

"Mark has called me several times since he's been gone, and he's mentioned you every time. He's never done that before, and now he's brought you home with him."

Betsy shook her head. "No, he only brought me

here because he was afraid I was in danger. He was only doing his job, keeping a witness safe."

Laura's forehead wrinkled, and she tilted her head to one side. "I think it's more than that. If you were just a witness, he would have had his office put you in a hotel room with guards at the door. Instead, he brings you home where you can see how he lives, eat the food he cooks and meet his sister. I'm telling you, Betsy, you're not just a witness to him."

Without saying more, Laura showed her to the room where she would be staying and left her alone to settle in. Betsy closed the door and sat down on the edge of the bed. She'd never been so confused in her life. Was she more than a witness to Mark? She thought she had known him, but now she realized she had no idea what he was really like.

She had accused him of caring only about his job, and now she understood what drove him in the pursuit of criminals. Then there was the sensitive man he kept hidden—the one who could create exquisite carvings from a block of wood. She'd seen glimpses of that man in the past few days when Mark had put his own life at risk to protect her.

The more she was with Mark, the more she realized she had never quit loving him. But that did her little good. If Mark's dedication to his job resulted from his parents' deaths, then she doubted if that would ever change. There was no chance he would ever feel about her like she did about him.

Still dressed in the clothes she'd worn when they left Ocracoke, she lay back on the bed and closed her eyes. Her last thought was of how hard it was going to be to keep him from seeing how she felt.

Mark heard Laura's footsteps as she entered the kitchen, but he didn't turn around. He placed the last utensil in the dishwasher, reached for a towel and dried his hands. Her silence told him volumes about what he could expect in the next few minutes. With a sigh, he forced himself to face her.

She leaned against the doorjamb, her arms crossed and an eyebrow cocked. A smirk pulled at her lips. "Just doing your job, huh?"

He folded the towel he still held and laid it on the counter. "I don't know what you're talking about."

She straightened to her full height and wagged a finger at him. "Oh, yes, you do. You told Betsy you were just doing your job keeping her safe. Why don't you tell her the truth?"

"And what do you think is the truth?" He leaned against the counter and crossed his arms.

"You're in love with her, Mark. Why can't you admit it?"

His heart dropped to the pit of his stomach, and he shook his head. "You're wrong, Laura."

Her eyes clouded, and she took a step closer to him. "Mark, I love you and want you to be happy. Why won't you let yourself?"

"You know why." He rubbed his fingers over his eyes as if he could erase the pictures that were still as vivid in his mind as they had been when he was twelve years old. "Mom died because of Dad's work. I made a vow years ago that I would never let my job put anybody I love in danger. That's why I stay away from you so much. I don't want to lead anybody to this house. I don't want you hurt, and I don't want that for Betsy, either."

She stepped closer and grasped his hand. "I know what it's like to lose out on happiness, Mark. My wedding was only two months away when Chet was killed while he was working undercover. I lost my parents and the man I loved to violence. I couldn't stand it if something happened to you, too."

"Nothing's going to happen to me."

"That's what Chet said, but it didn't stop a kid high on drugs from shooting him in the back. Why don't you get out of this kind of work? I know you want to. Dad wouldn't expect you to ruin your chance at happiness out of a misguided idea of being loyal to him." She paused for a moment. "You told me Betsy is a painter. You're a wood carver. The two of you have a lot in common besides a mutual attraction."

He shook his head. "Now I know you're wrong. Betsy doesn't think of me that way."

"Oh, yes she does. Take it from me. I can tell she's smitten."

He grinned and chucked her under the chin. "You're wrong, little sister. Don't worry about me. I'm the one who's supposed to take care of you. Like we said after Mom and Dad's funeral—just the two of us from now on."

"We were children then. Now we're adults, and there's room in our lives for other people. God's given you a great gift in Betsy. Don't miss this chance at happiness. It might not come again."

He put his hands on her shoulders and looked down at her. "And what about your chances at happiness? Are you ready to face losing Chet?"

Tears flooded her eyes, but she smiled. "I am. I've made some plans I want to tell you about while you're here, but we'll talk about that later. Now I need to get some sleep. I'm off for the next two days, which is good because it's the weekend. I hope you and Betsy will stay so I can get to know her better."

"I think that can be arranged. Now go on and get some sleep. After I check with the office, I'm going to take a nap. Then tonight I'll take you and Betsy out to my favorite restaurant for dinner. How does that sound?"

"It sounds great. I'll see you later."

He leaned over and kissed her on the cheek. Smiling, she walked from the room, but the words she'd spoken troubled him. How did she know he was in love with Betsy? He didn't think he was so obvious.

He pulled his cell phone from his pocket and dropped down into a chair at the table. There wasn't time to be thinking about his feelings for Betsy. He needed to know if the code had been broken and get his mind off Betsy.

It might sound like a simple thing to just think of something else, but it wasn't. Ever since he'd been on Ocracoke, he'd hardly been able to think of anything but being with Betsy. Maybe Laura was right. If this was his chance for happiness, he needed to take it before it was snatched from his grasp.

First, though, he had to make sure Betsy was safe from whoever wanted to kill her. After that, there would be time to decide if he wanted to take a chance on happiness or if he wanted to continue working undercover. He couldn't do both, and at the moment he had no idea which one he wanted most.

* * *

The weekend had passed too quickly. Now it was Sunday night, and they would be returning to Ocracoke the next morning. Betsy folded her arms across her stomach, leaned back in the patio table chair, and closed her eyes. It was so peaceful here in the backyard of Mark and Laura's house. It made her homesick for the tranquility she'd known on Ocracoke until a week ago. A gentle breeze blew across the patio and ruffled her hair. She sighed in contentment.

The last two days had been some of the most enjoyable she'd spent in a long time. Although she missed her family, she wished Mark could prolong his stay in Raleigh longer, but he couldn't. Mark hadn't exactly confirmed that the code on the flash drive had been broken, but from his long conversations on his cell phone yesterday and today, she guessed it had been. Now he was eager to get back to Ocracoke.

The back door of the house opened, and Mark and Laura emerged from the kitchen. Mark carried a tray containing glasses of iced tea, and Laura followed with dessert plates in one hand and the pound cake Mark had baked earlier in the other. Betsy still had trouble reconciling the man who seemed so at home in the kitchen with Mark's undercover appearance.

He set the tray down, handed her a glass of iced tea, and winked. "Laura made the tea, so I can't vouch for how good it is."

Laura placed the cake and plates on the table and propped her hands on her hips. "You'd better watch it, mister. I'll tell Betsy what a Casanova you were in high school and how you chased every girl in your class."

Mark's face turned crimson. He picked up a knife from the tray and cut a slice of cake. "Don't believe a word of what she says, Betsy. I didn't even date in high school."

Laura laughed and flopped down in the chair next to Betsy. "No, he didn't. I just wanted to see if he could still blush."

Betsy glanced from Mark to Laura and smiled. "It's been wonderful being here with you two. I'm going to miss you, Laura, when we go back to Ocracoke."

"Then you'll just have to come back. But if you want to see me again, you'd better come before Labor Day. I won't be here after that."

Mark had begun to cut another slice of cake, but he pulled the knife from the cake and stared at his sister. "What are you talking about?"

"I told you I had made some plans, and I suppose this is as good a time as any to tell you. I'm moving back to Memphis."

Mark scowled. "When you said you'd made

plans, I thought you meant you were ready to begin dating again. I didn't expect you to say you were moving. Why are you doing this?"

"For many reasons." Laura glanced at Betsy. "Mark went to work for the DEA just at the time I was graduating from nursing school. When he was assigned to Raleigh, he wanted me to join him, and I did. Now I spend most of my time alone here because Mark is seldom home."

Mark dropped into the chair next to Laura. "I call all the time, and I come home when I can."

"I know that, but it's not enough anymore. I want to go back home."

"B-b-but, that's eight hundred miles from here."

She smiled and laid her hand on his arm. "I know it is, but I need to do this. I need to get away from everything that reminds me of Chet and start my life over. I've prayed about this, and I know it's the right thing for me to do."

Mark fell back in his chair and continued to stare at her as if he still couldn't believe what she'd said. Betsy saw the concern on Mark's face and wished there was something she could say to ease his pain. Instead, she turned to Laura. "I'm happy for you, Laura. God will take care of you, and I wish you well in your new life."

"My new life," she murmured and glanced at Mark. "That's what we both need, Mark. I hope you'll think about the things I said to you about your own life. It's time to let the past go and live for the future."

He gritted his teeth and jumped to his feet. "Maybe it's easier for you to do than it is for me. I can't forget what happened in that driveway eighteen years ago."

Tears filled Laura's eyes. "Then I'll pray you'll find the strength to move past it and face a future free of that memory."

He didn't say anything for a moment, then he whirled and stormed into the house. Betsy watched him go and wished she could go after him, but it was best for him to be alone right now.

"I'm sorry I ruined your last night here, Betsy. I knew Mark would be upset when I told him what I planned to do, but I had to tell him."

"I hope you'll be happy with your decision, Laura."

She smiled. "There isn't a day that goes by that I don't think of Chet. No matter where I go, he's going to be with me, but God is helping me cope. In time, maybe the hurt will ease some."

Betsy wrinkled her brow and tilted her head to one side. "What did you mean by what you said about Mark needing to change his own life?"

"I don't know if Mark's told you this or not, but I know he wishes he could get out of law enforcement. He's only stayed in out of an obligation he feels he owes to our parents, but they would never want him to sacrifice his personal life the way he's done."

Betsy shook her head. "He's never said anything to me about leaving the DEA. Are you sure about that?"

Laura leaned forward and grabbed Betsy's hand. "I've tried to help you see the Mark very few people know while you've been here. He's not happy in his work anymore, and he's becoming burned out. That's dangerous for an agent. He's liable to become careless and think nothing can happen to him. I don't want him to end up dead like Chet. I can't lose someone else I love to violence."

Betsy swallowed back the fear that rushed through her. "I don't want that, either."

Laura squeezed her hand tighter. "Then help him, Betsy. Help him find his way to another life."

Betsy couldn't think of anything to say that would calm Laura's concern for Mark, so she smiled and nodded. Laura released her and reached for the piece of cake Mark had cut and passed it to her. The buttery cake almost melted in her mouth and brought to mind Laura's words about Mark's sensitive nature.

Over the past few days, Mark had become an enigma to her. She couldn't quite reconcile the gruff, uncaring Memphis agent she'd known with a man who enjoyed cooking for his family and friends. It was as if the two personalities within him were waging a heated battle to overcome the other. Like Laura, she hoped for the sensitive Mark to emerge the victor, but she had her doubts. His past had put a chokehold on him years ago, and he might never be able to break free.

TWELVE

Before leaving Raleigh, Betsy had confided in Laura how she dreaded reentering her studio, and the feeling hadn't subsided on the journey home. Now she stood in the doorway and scanned the room that had become like her second home. Anyone else entering the studio would be shocked to discover a life-and-death struggle had taken place here a few nights ago. She doubted if she could ever forget the terror she'd felt during those spine-chilling moments.

She concentrated on every detail of the room to see if there was any reminder that crime scene investigators had combed through the area. Everything appeared in order, and Treasury's staff had cleaned the room from top to bottom. The broken window had even been replaced in her absence. She inhaled deeply and started to enter, but the sound of the front door closing downstairs stopped her in her tracks.

The now familiar gait of footsteps on the hardwood entry hall told her Mark had returned from meeting with Brock and Scott. She waited for him to climb the stairs to his room, but he walked toward the kitchen instead. Eager to see him, she hurried downstairs. She found him sitting at one of the tables on the back porch with a cup of coffee in his hands.

She slid into the chair across from him. "How did the meeting with Brock and Scott go?"

"Okay. They've identified the dead guy through the National Crime Information Center. His name is Clive Warren. He has several convictions on drug-related charges and was suspected of working for a drug ring headquartered in St. Louis."

"Have they figured out who he was working with on Ocracoke?"

Mark shook his head. "No."

"What about the flash drive? Did they break the code?"

"Yeah. My supervisor told me the lab guys were able to do that. It contained financial records and names of places drugs were shipped to from Ocracoke."

Betsy breathed a sigh of relief. "That's great. Now all they have to do is raid those places and arrest the people there."

"It's not that simple." Mark set his coffee cup down on the table and wrapped his fingers around it. "We have agents keeping the places mentioned on the flash drive under surveillance. We still have to find out how the drugs are getting into the country."

"So your job here isn't over?"

"Not yet, but maybe we'll be able to solve this case yet. Brock and Scott questioned Luke Butler about Clive being in his gallery. He said he had only met the man a few days before we saw him there. His story is that Clive approached him about buying the gallery. He denied knowing Clive had a gun on him."

Betsy sat up straighter in her chair. "Do you think he's telling the truth?"

"I don't know." Mark took a sip of coffee and set the cup on the table. "We've suspected all along that there's some business on the island serving as a front for the smugglers. It could be Luke's gallery. I think I'll take him up on the offer to let me hang out there and observe him at work."

"That sounds like a good idea. I know you're going there on DEA business, but Luke is a very talented woodcarver. You could pick up some great techniques from watching him work."

Mark's forehead furrowed. "It wouldn't do me any good. I haven't carved anything in several years."

Betsy leaned forward and clasped her hands in front of her on the table. "I saw your carvings when we were in Raleigh. I've never seen such exquisite beauty. I think it would be a great stress reliever for you. You need to have something in your life besides chasing drug dealers."

Mark pushed to his feet and raked his hand through his hair. "Maybe you have a point, but I don't have time to think about that. I have to find whoever killed John and is after you."

She walked around the table and stopped in front of him. "I appreciate all you've done for me. And I'm glad you took me to meet Laura. I liked her a lot. She wants to get on with her life, and she wants you to do the same."

He shook his head. "Maybe someday, but not yet. There's still too much to do."

His words sucked the breath from her like a kick in the stomach. The trip to Raleigh might have been intended to keep her from danger, but it had set her up for heartbreak. She had come to care deeply for Mark and longed to have him return her feelings. From what he'd just said, there was no place in his life for anything—or anyone—except his self-imposed vendetta caused by his parents' deaths.

Sadness flickered in his eyes, and in that moment she knew he cared for her. She also recognized an unspoken truth. He would never voice those feelings. She took a bolstering breath and tried to smile.

"I know you don't think you can change the

person you are, but you can. Laura's found the strength through God's love to face her life. I hope you can do the same. Until that time, I'll be your friend, and I'll help you anyway I can."

He swallowed before he responded. "Thank you, Betsy. That means a lot to me."

She cleared her throat. "Now that we have that settled, how about us spending the afternoon at Luke's gallery? I would like to keep an eye on him, too. Besides, every time I watch him work, I learn something from him." She glanced at her watch. "Treasury's having dinner with some friends tonight, so I'll take you out to eat later to repay you for your hospitality this weekend."

He cocked an eyebrow. "You're not going to cook?"

She laughed. "Are you kidding? I thought I was a good cook until our trip to Raleigh. Now I don't feel like I'll ever be comfortable in a kitchen again."

He threw back his head and laughed. "So I surprised you, huh?"

She nodded. "You surprised me a lot."

His eyes darkened, and the muscle in his jaw twitched. "I may not be in that house a lot, but I still consider it my home. I'm glad you were there with me this weekend."

Her face warmed under his penetrating stare. Only a step, and she could be in his arms. But did he want it? She searched his face for an answer, and after a moment she backed away. "It was my pleasure. Now why don't we go to Luke's studio?"

She turned and walked to the back door. When she opened it, she glanced over her shoulder. He hadn't moved. He frowned, shook his head, and stuck his hands in his pockets. Then he ambled toward her. "Let's go."

Betsy nodded and led the way to his car in front of the bed-and-breakfast. As they drove toward Luke's studio, she studied Mark out of the corner of her eye. For years she'd harbored feelings that bordered on hate for the man she thought she'd known in Memphis. His short time on Ocracoke how shown her how wrong she'd been. She said a silent prayer to thank God for bringing him back into her life.

Maybe God's plan all along had been for her heart to be healed of hatred. Once she'd thought that impossible, but God had taken away those feelings. If He could do that, He could get her through the rough days after Mark left Ocracoke. And in time she would come to think of Mark as a man she'd loved and lost. All she had to do was place this situation in God's hands.

For the past three hours, Betsy had wandered around Luke's gallery and studied the pieces on display. She'd always known Luke possessed great skill when it came to mixing colors to achieve the effect he wanted, and now her respect for his talent had risen to a new high.

Luke had taken Mark into the back workroom soon after they arrived. The first hour or two had been fun talking to island visitors, but she was beginning to get hungry. She headed in the direction of the workroom but turned and glanced over her shoulder when the front door opened.

Mona Davis from the Ocracoke Health Center strolled into the shop and moved toward a display to her right. Betsy scanned Mona's face and arms for hints of bruises but didn't see anything. She remembered Mona's words about Mark being her boyfriend the last time they met, and she didn't want a repeat of that conversation. She started to turn away but remembered her words to Mona about how she would always be her friend. Taking a deep breath, she approached her.

"Hi, Mona. How are you today?" The carving Mona held slipped from her fingers, and Betsy caught it before it hit the floor. She chuckled and set the piece on the table. "I'm sorry. I didn't mean to startle you."

Mona's eyes grew large. "I—I guess I wasn't paying attention to what I was doing. I didn't expect to see you here, not after what happened to you a few nights ago."

Betsy rolled her eyes. "I guess everybody is talking about the man who attacked me in my studio."

Mona nodded. "I heard about it. How are you?"

"Fine. Lucky to be alive. It still scares me to think about it."

Mona's lips trembled, and she grasped Betsy's arm. "I'm so sorry, Betsy. You don't deserve something like that happening to you."

"Thank you for being concerned. I just hope Brock and Scott can find out who hired the hit man."

"I hope so, too." Mona took a deep breath. "Well, I'd better be going. It's nice to see you again." Mona turned and hurried toward the door. Before she stepped outside, she glanced back at Betsy. "Stay safe."

Betsy nodded. "Thanks. And remember what I said about being here for you if you ever need help."

"You're a good friend, Betsy."

Betsy stared at the door long after Mona had closed it and disappeared. There was something wrong with Mona today. She'd acted upset at Betsy's presence in the gallery. She shrugged and headed toward the door to the workroom. At the door to the workroom, a sudden thought jolted her to a stop.

Ever since the night she'd been attacked in her studio, Betsy had tried to figure out how the drug dealers had known she was the one who had the flash drive. At first she'd assumed the killers saw her at Springer's Point. If so, why hadn't they killed her, too? Even if they had seen Mark, they probably wouldn't have hesitated to kill both of them. But maybe they knew someone who could retrieve it later. Someone who worked at the place where the body would be taken.

Betsy slipped out the side door of the gallery into the parking lot and pulled her cell phone from her pocket. Her brother answered on the first ring. "Hello."

"Scott, this is Betsy. I've been thinking. Somebody had to know the flash drive wasn't on John Draper's body. They also had to know I was the one with him when he died. Did you and Brock question everybody who had access to his body?"

"We did. All along we've thought somebody who knew you had to pass on that information, but we can't figure out who it was. Arnold and the other EMT have worked with the deputies on Ocracoke for years, but we questioned them. We didn't come up with anything, though."

"What about Mona Davis? Did you question her?"

"Yeah. Again we didn't come up with anything.

But we're keeping a close watch on her and her boyfriend, Mac Cody."

"Do you think he's involved with the drug dealers?"

Scott exhaled. "We don't know."

"Have you talked with Mark about this?"

"Betsy, you don't need to get involved in…"

"I know you're only looking out for me," she interrupted. "But I'm already involved. More than I ever wanted to be. Thanks for the information. Bye."

Before Scott could respond, she ended the call. She stood in the parking lot for a few more minutes and debated what she should do. The thought that Mona might know something made Betsy want to shake her until she revealed who wanted her dead. But what if she was wrong and Mona knew nothing?

Betsy clenched her fists and grimaced. There was only one thing to do. She had to confront Mona about what she might know and appeal to her as a friend from childhood. Now all she had to do was convince Mark it was a good idea.

Mark glanced at the clock on the wall and shook his head. Had he really spent the entire afternoon bent over a table in the workroom of Luke Butler's gallery? In front of him, the body of a decoy was slowly beginning to take shape. Mark raised his arms over his head, stretched his back and smiled. He was tired, but it was a good feeling.

Behind him the door opened, and he glanced around to see Betsy entering the room. "How's it going?"

He pointed to the table. "It's beginning to look like a duck."

She laughed and plopped down in a chair across from him. "I peeked in on you a few times, but you were so engrossed in your work you didn't see me."

He chuckled and rubbed the back of his neck. "Yeah, I've really enjoyed this."

She crossed her arms and arched an eyebrow. "I could tell."

He picked up the block of wood with the outline of a duck's head drawn on it and held it out. "You observe the ducks around here all the time. Do you think I've got this right?"

She took the wood and studied the pattern. "This is really good, Mark. It's just right."

He smiled in satisfaction. "I'm glad you think so. Luke said it's very important to get the right attitude on the duck's head. It can mean the difference in whether or not your decoy will attract other birds."

"Yeah, that's what I've heard hunters say." She set the wood down and leaned forward. "While you've been in here having fun, I've been out in the gallery talking to Luke and the customers who've come in to shop," she whispered.

"Did you find out anything interesting?"

"Maybe," she said.

"What happened?"

She shook her head. "I don't want to tell you about it here. I'll tell you in the car. Are you ready to go?"

He stood and began to straighten up the work table. "Let me put some of this stuff away, and I'll be ready."

The door opened again, and Luke Butler walked into the room. "Leaving already, Mark?"

Betsy pushed to her feet. "I'm getting hungry, and I'm going to take Mark over to the Red Snapper for dinner."

Mark nodded and stuck out his hand. "Thanks, Luke, for all your help today. I'll come back tomorrow if that's okay."

Luke pumped his hand and grinned. "Make sure you do. It's been a long time since I've seen anybody with as much talent for carving as you have."

Mark's face grew warm, and he glanced at the floor. "Thanks, Luke, but it's just a hobby left over from my childhood."

The man's eyes narrowed. "Don't take it lightly, Mark. You've got a gift."

"You're right, Luke." Betsy grabbed Mark by

the arm and pulled him toward the door. "He'll be back tomorrow," she promised.

When they were in the car, Mark frowned and turned toward Betsy. "You must be starving to rush me out of there like that."

She snapped her seat belt in place and grinned. "I am…but that's not the reason I was in a hurry."

He listened as she told him about seeing Mona in the gallery. When she finished, he frowned. "I know Brock and Scott are keeping an eye on her. They'll let us know if she does anything suspicious."

"I know, but I want to talk to her myself."

"Why?" He glared at her. "Brock and Scott questioned her at length, but she insisted she didn't go near John's body. What makes you think she'll talk to you?"

"We've known each other since childhood, but today it was almost like she was ashamed to face me. I might be able to break through her defenses and get her to tell me what she knows."

"If she does know anything." Mark shook his head. "I don't like this, Betsy. You don't have any proof Mona is involved."

"Think about it, Mark. My caller at the British Cemetery already knew I had to be the one to have the flash drive. Somebody had to tell them. Besides the EMTs and Doc Hunter, Mona is the only other person who would have had access to John's body."

"I would be more inclined to think one of the EMTs was involved. After all, they searched the body at Springer's Point and said John had nothing on him."

"That's a possibility, but I have a gut feeling it's Mona. You didn't see how she acted with me. She was nervous, and I know she was hiding something. I need to talk to her again."

The determination in her eyes told him she wasn't going to give up. He held up his hands in surrender. "Okay, what do you want to do?"

"Everybody on the island knows each other's habits. Mona goes to the Blue Pelican after work every day and meets her boyfriend. After they've eaten, she usually goes home while he spends time hanging out with his friends. I think we should go the Red Snapper and eat dinner, then go to Mona's house and wait for her. When she gets there, I'll talk with her."

He shook his head. "Not alone."

"It will be better if you're not there. She would never talk in front of you."

He sighed. "And she probably won't with you, either."

"But I have to try."

Her chin quivered, and the small twitch of her lips made his heart slam against his chest.

He wished he could pull her into his arms and hold her until all her fears were gone. Instead, he grasped the steering wheel with one hand and the ignition with the other. The engine roared to life, and he pulled into the street. "Okay. We'll do it your way, but I won't be far away."

She settled back in her seat and stared ahead. He tried to ignore her presence, but he couldn't. Even though she'd been in danger, being with Betsy this last week had been the best time of his life. How could he ever go back to his lonely existence when this case was over? He'd pondered that question ever since he and Betsy had spent time with Laura. But he still hadn't arrived at an answer.

THIRTEEN

Betsy wished she could step out of the car and stretch her legs. She squirmed in her seat and swiveled to face Mark. He hadn't moved in the two hours they'd been sitting down the street from Mona's house. Probably the result of other long stakeouts he'd endured. His steady gaze appeared locked on Mona's house.

"I didn't think she'd be this long," Betsy said.

He didn't glance her way. "You never can tell what a suspect is going to do."

She smiled and cocked an eyebrow. "So now you're calling her a suspect?"

In the shadows she could see the grin on his face, but he didn't move. "I guess you caught me on that one."

Betsy let out a long breath and let her gaze drift over the dark houses up and down the street. "I never thought I would be involved in a stakeout with you."

"Oh, really? Is it not as much fun as you thought?"

She shook her head. "On the contrary, it's been nice sitting here with you. I feel like I finally understand my family of police officers."

"I'm glad you've enjoyed it." He paused for a moment but didn't look her way. "I've liked having you with me."

She waited for him to say more. When he didn't, she sighed and settled back in her seat. At that moment headlights appeared at the end of the street. She watched the approaching car slow down and turn into Mona's driveway.

"She's home," she whispered.

Betsy started to open the car door, but Mark reached out and stopped her. "Wait until she's inside."

"All right." She tried to contain her excitement as she watched Mona cross the yard and pause outside the front door before entering. Lights flooded the front room, and Betsy strained to catch a glimpse of Mona moving about. "I'm going now."

Mark caught her by the arm. "Are you sure you want to do this alone?"

"Yes."

"Then I'll wait here. But I'm warning you, if you're not back in thirty minutes, I'm coming after you."

"Okay."

Betsy stepped from the car and headed to the

front porch. The door opened the minute she knocked. "I thought you weren't coming. Why—" Mona stopped speaking, and her eyes grew large. "Betsy? What are you doing here?"

"I'd like to talk to you."

Mona cast a furtive glance past Betsy and then stepped aside. "Okay. Come on in, but this really isn't a good time for me…"

Betsy walked into the room and waited for Mona to close the door. "The last few days haven't been good for me either, Mona. Can you imagine what it's like being targeted by killers? I've had three attempts on my life."

Mona swallowed and bit down on her lip. "I know it must have been terrible. I'm really sorry about what's happened to you."

"Are you?"

"Of course I am."

Betsy stared into the face of the woman she'd known all her life and sent a silent plea to God for the words to speak. She stood in danger of losing a lifelong friend if she was wrong. If she was right, however, she'd lost Mona's friendship a long time ago. She had to find out the truth, and something told her Mona held the key.

"Mona, I really thought we were friends. We have a lot of history together. We were in the same class at school, and we attended church together."

"I know," Mona said. "Your mother was our Sunday school teacher."

"Yes, and she always loved you. Do you remember the dress she made for you when your mother was expecting your sister? She wanted you to have a new dress for Easter like all the other girls, and your mother had been put on bed rest until she gave birth."

Mona smiled. "It was a white cotton dress with pink flowers on it. I felt like a princess in it."

"Then later, when your father was killed in that fishing accident, my father gave your mother a job at the sheriff's headquarters on Ocracoke. We played there many afternoons after school and planned what we were going to do when we grew up."

Mona glanced down at her watch. "I remember, but I really don't have time for a trip down memory lane. Get to the point, Betsy."

"All right. The thing that bothers me is that I thought we were friends. But friends don't pass along information that almost gets someone killed."

Mona's face turned white. "What are you talking about?"

Betsy took a step closer. "I wondered why people were trying to kill me, and then I found the flash drive. They thought I had it because they knew it wasn't on John Draper's body. They knew it because you told them."

"What?" Mona looked shocked. "You're out of your mind."

There was no going back now. Betsy was committed to following up on her accusation, and she had to push Mona harder. She gritted her teeth and took another step forward. "I know you were the one. What have I ever done to you that made you want me to be killed?"

Mona's eyes filled with tears, and she shook her head. "I didn't want you to be killed."

"Then why did you tell?" An idea popped into her head. "Maybe you told because you were threatened, too. Was it Mac? Did he make you do this?"

Tears streamed down Mona's face. "Please…"

"No," Betsy snapped. "I want to know what made you put me in danger of being killed."

Mona collapsed on the sofa and buried her face in her hands. Her body shook with sobs. "I didn't know you would be hurt. Mac just said some friends of his needed to get a flash drive that was probably hidden on the man's body. He told me I had to get it for him or he would be in big trouble."

Betsy eased down next to Mona. "Then you did tell him."

Mona looked up at Betsy with stricken eyes. "Yes, but I didn't know what they would do. When I heard what had happened at the general store and then at your studio, I confronted Mac about it. He said if I didn't want the same thing to happen to me, I'd keep quiet."

Betsy grasped Mona's hands and squeezed. "Who are these friends?"

"I don't know, and that's the truth. He wouldn't tellme."

Betsy placed her fingers under Mona's chin and raised her face until they stared into each other's eyes. "This is very important, Mona. There are drugs being smuggled onto this island. That means that people's lives all across the country are going to be ruined because a few men want to make money. You don't want that on your conscience. Is Mac involved?"

Mona's lips puckered, and she nodded. "He is… but I don't know who they are."

"How are the drugs getting on the island?"

"I overheard Mac and another guy talking one night about drugs that are attached to the hulls of ships coming up the coast from South America. Divers meet them at sea where they get the drugs and transport them back here where they're smuggled onto the mainland."

"How are they smuggled?"

Mona shook her head. "I don't know. I only know that much because of what I heard."

"Do you know when they're expecting the next shipment?"

"I'm not sure, but I suspect it's tonight. Mac told me he couldn't come over tonight because he has to work. That usually means he's got a shipment to unload."

Betsy smiled. "Thanks, Mona. You've been a great help. This information will help Brock and Scott a lot."

Mona began to cry again. "What am I going to do? If Mac and his friends find out I told you this, they're going to be furious."

Betsy stood and pulled Mona to her feet. "You've got to get off the island. Go to your sister's house in Greenville and stay there until Brock and Scott catch these people. Can you do that?"

Mona thought for a moment before she nodded. "I'll get paid tomorrow at noon. As soon as I get my check, I'll get on the ferry."

"No, you have to go before that." She reached in her purse, pulled out some bills and pressed them into Mona's hands. "Take this money. I'll have Doc send your check to your sister's house. You make sure you're on the first ferry in the morning."

Mona stared at the money she held. "I can't take this."

"Yes, you can. I want you safe."

Mona threw her arms around Betsy and hugged her. "Thank you. I've almost been out of mind with guilt because of what's happened. I'm sorry I caused you a problem."

"I know. Now take care of yourself, and I'll talk to you soon."

Betsy patted Mona on the shoulder and hurried out of the house. She ran to Mark's car and climbed in. "You were gone so long I was getting ready to come after you," he growled. "Did you find out anything?"

As he drove toward Treasury's house, she related everything Mona had said. "We have to let Brock know this right away."

Mark nodded. "I'll take you back to Treasury's and make sure you're safe. Then I'll go to headquarters. I think Brock and Scott are on duty tonight. We'll scour this island and see if we can find where the drugs are being unloaded."

The thought of Mark, Scott and Brock being in danger sent a shiver through her. What would she do if something happened to any of them? She glanced toward Mark, and her heart constricted at the determined look on his face. She'd seen him like that in Memphis the night the police raided the restaurant. He'd been on the trail of drug dealers then just like now. If he was successful on Ocracoke, he would soon leave.

That would be better than having him dead or injured by the men he was after. She closed her eyes and prayed God would keep her loved ones safe.

The car came to a stop, and she opened her eyes. They were back at Treasury's, and Mark had turned to stare at her. "Are you all right?" he asked.

She smiled. "Yes. Be careful tonight, Mark. I'll be praying for you."

His face showed no expression as they walked toward the house. She wished she and Mark could be like a normal couple who had gone to dinner and were returning home. Instead, he would leave in a few minutes to look for men who wouldn't hesitate to kill to protect their illegal goods.

She wanted to throw her arms around him and beg him to stay with her, but it would do no good. Mark had always made it clear his job came first. All she could do was accept his choice and learn to live with it.

Mark sat in a chair next to the dispatcher's desk at the sheriff's headquarters on Ocracoke and drained the last drop of coffee from his mug. It had been a long night, and he needed some sleep. He, Brock and Scott had combed the island ever since he'd told them of Betsy's meeting with Mona, but they had found no evidence of anybody bringing drugs ashore. They had no idea where to look next.

The horn from the departing ferry drifted from the direction of the harbor, and he breathed a sigh of relief. Mona Davis should be on her way to safety.

Lisa, who was the dispatcher on duty, glanced up from her computer and smiled. "Scott called a few minutes ago. He's bringing some muffins from The Coffee Shop in a little while."

"Good. Is he planning to go home and get some rest then?"

Lisa shrugged. "I don't know what my husband and Brock will do. They'll probably stick around, even though we have two other officers on patrol this morning."

The door opened, and Scott hurried inside. "Lisa, where's Brock?"

"He's out at the wild pony corral. They had some horses get out last night. Why?"

Scott glanced at Mark. "I just watched the ferry leave. Mona Davis wasn't on board."

Mark pushed to his feet. "Are you sure?"

"Yeah. I think we'd better check on her." He glanced at Lisa. "Call Brock and tell him to meet us at Mona's house."

Without waiting for a reply, they ran from the office, jumped in Scott's squad car and roared toward Mona's house. They screeched to a stop at the front walk.

Mark frowned. "I don't like this. Her car is parked exactly where it was when Betsy and I were here last night."

They jumped from the car and raced to the porch. Scott pounded on the front door. "Mona, are you in there? Open up. It's Scott Michaels."

When there was no answer, he glanced at Mark. "Should we go in or wait for Brock?"

"Something may have happened to her. We need to check. Don't worry—I'll pay for the door if she's all right."

Before Scott could protest, Mark drew his leg back and crashed his foot against the door panels with all his weight behind the force. The door splintered, but his second kick knocked the door off its hinges. Scott pushed the sagging door aside, and they pulled out their guns.

Mark wrapped both hands around his gun and extended his arms in front of him. A deathly silence filled the room. "I don't hear anything. That noise should have caused some kind of response from anybody inside the house."

Scott's fingers tightened on his weapon. "Yeah. That's what worries me." He inched forward. "Police!" he yelled. "We're coming in."

Scanning the room, Mark eased through the doorway behind Scott into the living room. No light filtered through the closed curtains, giving the room a ghostly appearance. "Mona, are you here?" Mark called out.

"Hello!"

The shrill word ricocheted off the walls and hardwood floors. Mark tightened his grip on his gun and darted a glance at Scott. "Mona," Scott yelled. "Is that you?"

"Hello!"

Mark pointed to a door standing slightly ajar down the hallway. "It's coming from there," he whispered.

Scott took a step, and the floor creaked. The sound sent a chill up Mark's back. Experience had taught him to never assume anything but be prepared for anything when entering a strange area. They had no idea what awaited them in that room.

Mark flattened himself against the wall and slid toward the door. A sound like someone scratching on wood drifted through the opening. With his gun trained on the door, he took a deep breath and yelled. "This is the police. Come out with your hands up."

"Come in."

A bewildered look flash across Scott's face, and he glanced at Mark. "Ready?"

Mark nodded, inched closer and kicked the door open. It crashed against the bedroom wall, and a picture hanging in the hallway tumbled to the floor. Sweeping his gun in front of him, Mark charged into the room and came to a sudden stop. Scott plowed into his back.

A shrill cry from the corner of the room split the air. "I'm a pretty bird," the voice called out.

Mark exhaled a long breath and relaxed his grip on the gun. In the dim light, he could make out a large birdcage sitting atop a corner table. He took a step closer and squinted. Inside the cage the biggest parrot he'd ever seen paced back and forth on his perch and eyed them suspiciously.

Scott chuckled and lowered his gun. "That bird nearly scared me to death."

"Me, too." Mark reached for the switch on the wall, and light flooded the room. His gaze raked the room, and he sucked in his breath at the sight of Mona lying motionless on the floor in a pool of blood beside the birdcage. "Here she is." Mark dropped down beside her and felt for a pulse. "She's still alive. Call for help."

Mona stirred, and her eyes fluttered open. "Help me," she whispered.

Mark squeezed her hand. "Don't worry. Help is on the way. Can you tell me who did this?"

She licked her lips and frowned. "Mac." She closed her eyes and gasped. "Caught me about to leave."

Mark leaned closer. "Stay with me, Mona. The

EMTs will be here any minute. Did you tell Mac about Betsy's visit?"

"Y-yes. He hit me and I fell. That's all I remember."

Mark looked up at Scott. "Did you hear that?"

He nodded. "I'll tell Lisa to alert our deputies to be on the lookout for Mac."

Sirens wailed in the distance, and Mark turned his attention back to Mona. "Hang on, Mona. They're almost here."

There was no response, and Mark bent over her. "She's still breathing," he said. At that moment Arnold and his partner rushed into the room.

Mark and Scott backed into the hallway and let the men work on their patient. Minutes later, Arnold appeared in the doorway. "We're going to transport her to the health center. Doc's already called for the helicopter. She needs to get to a hospital as soon as possible. That nasty wound in the back of her head appears to have been caused by being struck with something. We'll know more when we get her to the mainland."

"Is she going to live?" Scott asked.

"I don't know," Arnold said. "I hope so. I've worked with Mona for several years. I sure would hate to lose her."

Scott and Mark waited until the EMTs had left before they reentered the bedroom. Mona's packed suitcases sat beside the bed, and the nightstand lay on its side on the floor. Scott pointed to the dresser. Several framed photographs lay on the floor beside it. "It looks like a struggle took place in here."

Mark nodded and leaned closer to examine the corner of the table with the birdcage. Traces of blood covered the edge, and several hairs appeared stuck to the wood. "It looks like she might have hit her head here." He pointed to the floor beside her body. "Did you see this? It looks like her attacker stepped in the blood and left his footprint."

Scott bent over and studied it. "Yeah. I'll take some pictures of this. Then I'll get some evidence bags and collect some samples. Want to help process this crime scene? I'm afraid we don't have any hired investigators in our county to do it for us."

Mark chuckled. "Glad to help... I've done it lots of times before. But if you don't mind, I'd like to call Betsy first. She'll be upset if she hears about Mona from somebody else."

He stepped into the living room, punched in Betsy's number, and waited for her to answer. "Hello," she said.

Mark smiled at the groggy sound of her voice. "Did I wake you?"

"No. I was awake, but I haven't had my coffee yet. Did you find the drugs?"

"No, but there's something else I wanted to tell you."

She listened while he told her of the recent events. When he'd finished, he heard a soft sob. "This is all my fault. I should never have gone to her house."

"I'm sorry about Mona, too, but this isn't your fault. Because of you, we now know where we need to look. As soon as Mac is picked up, we may be able to get to the bottom of this whole case."

"I hope so. I want it to be over…and I want Mona to be all right."

Her voice broke on the last word, and his heart lurched. If only there was something he could do to make her feel better. "Hey," he said. "You didn't tell me Mona had a parrot."

"Oh, yeah. She keeps it in her bedroom. I didn't see it last night."

He chuckled. "Well, Scott and I saw it."

By the time he had finished the story of how he and Scott had almost shot an innocent bird, she was giggling uncontrollably. The sound of it made him smile. She gasped for breath. "Oh, Mark, I can hardly wait to tease Scott about this. Mona would never have forgiven you if you'd killed Pedro." Then she paused, and when she spoke again, her tone was once more serious. "That is if Mona lives. I hope she does."

"So do I. All we can do now is pray."

She didn't reply right away. When she spoke, he detected a hint of surprise in her words. "Will you pray, Mark?"

Only then did he realize what he'd said and how natural it had seemed. "I've been thinking ever since we went to Raleigh. You and Laura think praying works for you. If it does, I need to give it a try. I want to know more about the peace both of you find in your faith. Will you help me, Betsy?"

"I will. Nothing would make me happier, and I'm sure it would Laura, too."

"Then we'll talk later. Until I get back to Treasury's, though, I want you to stay there. Don't go anywhere. Okay?"

"Okay, Mark. I'll see you later, and be careful."

"I will," he whispered and disconnected the call.

He stared at the phone and thought about everything that had happened since he arrived on Ocracoke. John's death, the attempts on Betsy's life and now the attack on Mona had taken a toll on him. But nothing had affected him as much as hearing Betsy and his sister talk about their faith. If it worked for the two women he loved most in the world, then he wanted it, too.

He walked out the front door of Mona's house into the yard and stared up at the sky. A few dark clouds, threatening rain, dotted the horizon. "God, most of the time I feel like those clouds. Like a storm's brewing in my body. But I don't want to feel that way anymore. Do You really care about me? If You do, help me find peace," he prayed.

His eyes closed. The wind had grown stronger, and it blew the scent of the roses planted beside Mona's house in his direction. It was as if the flowers spread their sweet aroma through his soul and left him feeling at peace with himself and the world. The picture of his parents' lifeless bodies rose up in his mind, but he felt no anger. Instead he remembered how they'd told Laura and him how much they loved them before they left that fateful morning.

That was what he needed to hold on to. Not the violence that took them from him. For the first time since he was twelve years old, he knew he could now face their deaths and embrace a new life like Laura had spoken about. Most of all, he wanted Betsy to be a part of that life. He had to convince her to give him a chance to prove how much he loved her. Then maybe she would love him, too.

FOURTEEN

Mark paced back and forth in the break room of the Ocracoke sheriff's office. He wished he could be in Brock's office right now helping interrogate Mac Cody, but he couldn't. As far as he knew, the drug gang on the island still hadn't figured out he was an undercover officer, and he wanted to keep it that way.

Waiting hadn't been easy, though. From time to time one of them would open the door and peek into the break room to inform him of what was going on with Mac. So far, he'd insisted he'd spent the night at a friend's house and hadn't been to Mona's house this morning.

The door opened, and Lisa walked into the room. "I thought I'd check on the coffeepot. I can't let it get empty or Scott has a fit."

Mark nodded. "I poured the last cup a little while ago. I should have made some more."

She waved her hand in protest. "No, I don't mind. Besides, it looks like we may be here a long time. Mac's not talking, and Brock's determined to make him." She sighed and glanced at her watch. "None of you ate any lunch, and I know you have to be hungry. I need to run to the Sandwich Shop and pick us up some food before the storm hits."

Mark walked to the window and looked out. Even though it was early afternoon, the sky already looked dark. "I saw the clouds earlier. Have they gotten closer?"

"Oh, yeah. We have bad storm warnings out. This one is moving westward, and they're predicting high tides on the Pamlico Sound side of the island. A lot of the tourists are leaving. The line for the ferry that just left was long. I expect we'll see an even longer line at four o'clock when the last one for the day leaves."

His stomach growled, and he grinned. "I guess I'm hungrier than I thought. A hamburger would hit the spot. Thanks for thinking of me, Lisa."

She smiled. "I take care of all the guys around here. Happy to add one more." She glanced over her shoulder as she headed for the door. "By the way, Doc called. Mona's in intensive care at the mainland hospital. She has a bad concussion, and some bleeding around her brain. But she's holding her own."

"That's a little good news. Maybe it'll get better."

Lisa closed the door, and he walked back to the

window. If the dark clouds in the distance and the wind rustling the leaves on the trees were any indication, they were in for a downpour. He strode to a television across the room and scrolled through the channels until he found a station devoted to weather. The news for the eastern seaboard focused on the approaching storm, and he settled on the couch to watch.

According to the announcers, the severest part of the storm was tracking straight up the Pamlico Sound and should arrive on the island in a few hours. He glanced at his watch and thought of what Lisa had said about the lines for the last ferry. He wondered if the smugglers would be in the vehicles waiting to board at four o'clock. They might very well be if Mac didn't break soon and tell them where the drugs were hidden.

It pained him to think of the lives that would be impacted if the smugglers were successful—dealers, users and their families, and police officers trying to stem the illegal flow into the country. For the second time that day, he bowed his head and prayed for Brock and Scott to be successful.

Betsy hadn't been able to work all day. Every time she tried to concentrate on her latest painting, her thoughts turned to Mona, and guilt flooded through her. Her visit to Mona's house last night had to be the cause of what happened.

If Mona died, Betsy didn't know how she could face it. She needed to get her mind on something else. She sighed, threw down the paint brush, and strode to the television across the room.

As she flipped through the channels, a news report of a storm approaching the island caught her attention. She turned the volume up and dropped down in her desk chair. An uneasy feeling rippled through her at the forecaster's dire warning for islanders. The predicted storm promised to be the worst of the summer.

She ran to the window, pulled back the curtain and scanned the horizon. In the distance the dark sky supported the TV report. Her eyes widened at a sudden thought. In all the excitement of the last few days, she'd forgotten Will said their shipment to the Raleigh gallery would leave on the last ferry today. She wondered if he had heard the weather report. Maybe she should call him. The last time they sent a shipment when it was raining, water had leaked through a crack in the truck's back door and damaged one of her paintings. She didn't want that to happen again.

She pulled her cell phone from the pocket of the baggy capris she'd put on that morning and groaned. When she'd come home last night from Mona's, she must have forgotten to put her phone on the charger, because now the battery was dead. Why hadn't she noticed how low it was when

Mark called earlier? She'd have to use the bed-and-breakfast's phone.

She dashed down the stairs to Treasury's office but skidded to a stop at the door. A man's voice thundered inside the room. "What do you mean you're all booked for tonight?"

Betsy recognized the tone of a man who Treasury had described as a very demanding guest. She inched closer and peeked into the room. "I can't call back later. I'm going out for a few hours, and I'm having trouble getting cell phone service anywhere on this island. I'm on the landline at the place where I'm staying, and I'm not hanging up until I get an answer." He paused a minute before he spoke again. "I'll wait while you check. I'm sure you can find a table for me tonight if you try."

Betsy glanced at her watch and frowned. She doubted if Treasury's guest would give up his call long enough for her to use the phone. Throwing up her hands in despair, she turned and ran from the house. It would only take a few minutes to go to the gallery and check the shipment. She could be there and back before anybody knew she was gone.

She jumped in her car and reached for the ignition. Mark's warning about not leaving her studio flashed in her mind, and she bit down on her lip. But he had meant for her not to go out in public.

Will's gallery was a different matter. Besides her studio, it was probably the safest place for her to be. Will would be there, and they could check the crates together before they were loaded on the truck.

She glanced at the approaching clouds one more time and made her decision. Mark might not like her going out, but she would deal with that later. Right now her paintings and their safe arrival at the Raleigh gallery were her primary concerns. She pressed down on the accelerator and pulled into the street.

She glanced in the rearview mirror a few moments later and spotted a black car pulling out from the street that ran beside Treasury's house. A half block from Treasury's house, she braked at a four-way stop and watched as the car approached from behind. A warning rippled through her body. The memory of cold fingers closing around her throat sent an icy chill through her. Maybe she should have done as Mark said and stayed at her studio. Was she being followed? There was only one way to find out.

At the next street instead of turning toward Will's gallery, she headed straight through the village and out the road toward the beach ramp. Ignoring the fifteen mile per hour village speed limit, she sped through town. Just as she reached the outskirts, she caught sight of the black car several blocks behind her.

As she accelerated, she searched her mind for some way to lose the trailing car. Ahead she spotted Swanson's Campground and drove through the entrance. Hoping she couldn't be seen from the road, she pulled into a parking space on the far side of the small building that served as Mr. Swanson's office and waited. From where she sat, she had a good view of the highway.

Within seconds, the black car sped by but didn't turn into the campground. Betsy tried to catch a glimpse of someone inside, but all she could make out was that the driver wore sunglasses and a baseball cap. She waited a few minutes, then pulled onto the road and headed toward the village.

Her hands trembled and she gripped the steering wheel. She had no proof the car had been following her. It could have been a coincidence they were going in the same direction. As soon as she checked on her paintings, she would go back to the studio and not budge until Mark returned.

When she pulled into the parking lot of Will's gallery, the Closed sign hung inside the front door. He always closed on the afternoons he loaded his pottery and her paintings on the truck bound for the mainland. She pulled around the building and came to a stop at the back of his studio. A panel truck sat near the porch, its back door open. Inside Betsy could see several crates that had already been loaded. She ran to the porch and pounded on the door.

"Will, let me in!"

The door opened, and Will stood there, a shocked expression on his face. "Betsy, what are you doing here?"

"Did you know there's a storm coming?"

He nodded. "Yes. We're trying to hurry with the loading so we can make the last ferry before the storm hits."

"I thought I'd check to make sure my paintings are packed better this time." She stepped forward.

He smiled and moved aside. "Maybe you'd better check them out."

He closed the door behind her as she walked into the studio. Several men she'd never seen before were packing wrapped pieces of Will's pottery in crates. One of them glanced up, and his eyebrows arched. His gaze shifted to Will, who gave a slight nod.

The silence that hung over the room sent goose bumps up her arm. Something wasn't right here. She glanced around and spotted several long, flat boxes sitting on the work table. A young man who hadn't noticed her arrival reached into one of them and pulled out a plastic bag filled with a white powder. He looked up as he handed the bag to the taller man, and his mouth dropped open.

Betsy frowned and turned to Will. "What are they doing?"

He smiled. "Packing the shipment to the gallery."

She shook her head. "But what's in that bag he's putting in the crate?"

"What do you think it is?"

The truth hit Betsy like a slap in the face, and she shrank away from Will. "Cocaine?"

He nodded. "I always thought you were a smart girl, Betsy. You should have been smart enough to have given us the flash drive. Where is it?"

Betsy staggered backward and gaped at Will, the man she had worked with and trusted for two years. How could he be involved in the plot to kill her? But it all made sense. Mark had said they thought the smugglers were using an island business as a front for their shipments. And how better to avoid suspicion than to use the work of a family member of the island lawmen?

"How could you? I thought you were my friend."

"I'll ask once more. Where is the flash drive?" he asked through clenched teeth.

She lifted her chin and glared at him. "In the hands of the DEA, and they'll stop you."

Rage filled his face, and he advanced on her. "They have to catch me first."

Panic-stricken at the anger flashing in his eyes, Betsy turned and ran for the door. Just as she reached for the knob, the door swung open. A man wearing sunglasses and a baseball cap blocked her exit. Before she could move, he grabbed her arms, swung her around to face Will, and marched her back into the room.

"What do you want me to do with her, Boss?" he growled.

Will stroked his chin and stared at her. After a moment, he shook his head and sighed. "Betsy, you could have spared me making this decision if you'd just cooperated at the beginning. You've always been too stubborn for your own good." He smiled as a rumble of thunder drifted into the room. "The forecast says we're in for a bad storm and high tides. Since Betsy enjoys being with the birds out on the Sound, I think we should give her the pleasure of seeing a storm up close. Tie her up and put her in one of the curtain blinds on the Sound, but tear the curtain off before you leave. We want to make sure the water takes care of her."

"No!" Betsy screamed. "You can't leave me out there to drown." Tears streamed down her face. "I thought you were my friend."

He shrugged and nodded to the man holding her. "Now get her out of here. We'll get rid of her car and finish up here so the truck can make the four o'clock ferry. Then we'll all leave this island on my boat."

The man put his arm around her waist and picked her up. Betsy strained against his arms and kicked with all her might. "Hey," he yelled. "I need some help here. Somebody grab her legs."

One of the other men dashed across the room and grabbed her legs, but she continued to writhe and twist. In the struggle she felt something slip from her pocket. Her phone with its cover of brightly colored swirling flowers and butterflies tumbled to the floor. Her heart thudded as the phone landed underneath a table. The thought that she should have called Mark before leaving Treasury's flashed in her mind, and she twisted in her captor's grip again.

The third man rushed up beside her and wrapped a piece of rope around her legs. She winced as he pulled the rope tight, and she groaned as another rope circled her wrists and tied them behind her back. Then they dropped her to the floor where she landed facedown. The impact stunned her for a moment, and the taste of blood filled her mouth.

Will knelt beside her, a piece of cloth in his hand. "I hope you enjoy your day on the water, Betsy."

He wrapped the cloth around her mouth and tied it at the back of her head. When he stepped away and turned his back, two of the men picked her up, carried her outside, and tossed her into the backseat of the black car she had seen following her earlier.

As the car began to move, Betsy forced herself to breathe deeply. She'd heard her family discuss many times how important it was to collect details that might lead to the capture of a criminal. After a moment, despair welled up in her. Why was she kidding herself? Nobody knew where she was. She should never have left without letting Mark know. Even after she realized the black car was following her, she should have driven to the police station instead of to Will's studio. Her independent nature had really gotten her in trouble this time, and she felt more alone than she'd ever been in her life.

Just like at the general store when she'd been taken hostage, her mother's face materialized in her mind. Her mother might not be with her any longer, but the faith she'd instilled in Betsy still ruled her life.

She closed her eyes and prayed for strength to face what lay ahead.

Mark swallowed the last bite of the hamburger Lisa had brought him. He hadn't seen Brock or Scott in the last thirty minutes, and he wondered what was going on in the interrogation room. He stood up and ambled over to the window. The sky had grown darker, and thunder rumbled in the distance.

The door opened, and he turned to see Scott striding into the room. A big grin lit his face. "We got a call from Sheriff Baxter's office on the mainland. Mona regained consciousness about an hour ago and was able to give a statement to one of our officers. She told him how Mac threatened to kill her when he found her leaving. He hit her and she fell."

Mark nodded. "Good. So have you told Mac this?"

"Yeah, that and the fact that we have his footprint in the blood on Mona's bedroom floor finally broke him. He's facing attempted-murder charges. We told him we'd see what we could do to help if he came clean about the drugs."

"Did he?"

"He gave it all up, told us how he met the divers out at the beach last night and took the containers of drugs to their destination here on the island."

Mark's heart kicked against his chest. "Did he tell you where he took them?"

Scott smiled. "He sure did, even told us the name of the guy who's the head man on the island. Will Cardwell."

Mark could hardly believe his ears. "Will Cardwell, Betsy's friend?"

Scott chuckled. "One and the same. And the drugs are leaving the island this afternoon. Some are going in a shipment of Will's pottery, but some are going by car. He has no idea who's transporting by car, though."

Mark glanced at his watch. "It's three-thirty now. We need to get down to the ferry and stop that truck of Will's before it gets on board. As for the cars, we'll have to search them. Can you get a drug dog over here from the mainland?"

A loud clap of thunder split the air and rattled the windows in the room. Scott ran to the window and peered out. "It looks like the storm is about to hit full force. To get a dog here in time, we'd have to bring him over on a helicopter. It doesn't look like that's going to happen in this weather."

Mark raked his hand through his hair and groaned. "Then we'll have to try and figure out which car it is. Are you and Brock finished with Mac?"

"Yeah. He's in a cell. Brock was talking with one of the other deputies when I came in here. He's sending him to keep an eye on Will's studio, and Larry Hamilton, the other one on duty, is going to the ferry to help us."

"Let me know when you're ready," Mark called out as Scott hurried from the room. "I want to check on Betsy and tell her what we've found out."

He punched in Betsy's number and waited

for her to answer. After a few rings, it went to voice mail. He pulled the phone from his ear and frowned. Why wasn't she answering? He waited a few minutes and dialed again. Her voice mail kicked on right away. He ended the call and punched in the number for the bed-and-breakfast. Treasury answered on the first ring.

"Island Connection Bed-and-Breakfast. May I help you?"

"Treasury, this is Mark. I've called Betsy's cell phone several times, but she's not answering. Do you know if she's in her studio?"

"I haven't seen her since lunch when she went upstairs. She's probably busy and has her phone turned off."

Mark pursed his lips. "I need to talk to her. Will you tell her to call me?"

"I'll be glad to do that. I'll go upstairs in a few minutes."

"Thanks, Treasury. I appreciate it."

He disconnected the call just as the door opened. Scott stuck his head in and smirked. "Are you ready to bust some drug dealers?"

Mark nodded. "I've waited for this day for months. I only wish John could be here with us."

He followed Scott and Brock out the front door and climbed into Scott's squad car. As they rode to the ferry terminal, excitement overtook him. It was always this way when a long case was about to end. He just had to make sure nothing went wrong and jeopardized months of work.

As they neared the boarding area for the ferry, rain began to hit the roof of the car. He stared out the window at the wind blowing through the trees. Apparently they were going to get wet. His thoughts were interrupted by the ringing of his cell phone. He pulled it from his pocket. "Hello."

"Mark, this is Treasury. I can't find Betsy anywhere. She's not in her studio."

His stomach knotted with fear. "Did you see her leave?"

"No, but I looked outside, and her car is gone." A sob cut off the last word. "Oh, Mark, where is she and why would she have left?"

"I don't know, Treasury. But don't worry. Scott and I will find her. If she comes home before we get there, make her stay."

"I will, even if I have to tie her to a chair."

He disconnected the call and glanced at Scott. "Betsy's not at Treasury's."

Scott's face grew white. "Why would she go out when there's a bad storm coming in?"

Mark clenched his fists. "I don't know."

He wanted to tell Scott to turn the car around so they could find Betsy, but he couldn't. They had a job to do right now, and finding Betsy would have to wait. Out of the corner of his eye he saw Scott's lips move, and he knew Betsy's brother had just sent a plea to God for the safety of his sister.

Ahead Mark could see the cars lined up waiting to board the ferry. Scott sped past the vehicles and skidded to a stop at the front of the line. Brock pulled in behind him, and another squad car rolled to a stop beside them. The ferry sat at its berth ready to begin boarding.

Brock jumped out and ran to Scott's car. "I'll tell the captain there's going to be a delay. The truck from Will's gallery is about halfway back in line. Block it in with the squad cars so they can't get away."

Scott radioed the other car and within seconds the truck was surrounded. Without taking time to don any rain gear, Mark and Scott jumped out, their guns trained on the driver of the vehicle. The rain splattered against Mark as he stepped outside, but he didn't hesitate. He ran to the truck, jerked the door open and pointed his gun at the man behind the wheel.

"Get out and place your hands on the side of the truck!" A look of panic flashed across the man's face. Mark took a step closer. "Now!"

The man climbed out, turned, and pressed his hands against the side of the truck. Scott grabbed his arms and cuffed his hands behind his back. Deputy Hamilton pulled the keys from the ignition and within seconds had unlocked the back door of the truck and had climbed inside.

Rain trickled down Mark's face, but he didn't move. He wiped it out of his eyes and kept his gun trained on his prisoner. It only took a few minutes before he heard what he'd been waiting months to hear. "I found cocaine. Lots of it. And that's only in the first crate."

Scott stepped up to the prisoner. "It looks like you're under arrest, mister." He took the man by the arm and marched him to the squad car. "You have the right to remain silent…"

Mark heard Scott read the prisoner his rights, but he couldn't concentrate. He stared at the long line of cars waiting to board the ferry. One of those vehicles also contained drugs. But how was he going to figure out which one it was?

Brock ran up at that moment. "The ferry captain says the worst part of this storm hasn't hit yet. He wants to leave as soon as possible so he can stay ahead of it. Any idea on which cars we should start searching?"

Lightning flashed overhead, and the trees at the edge of the boarding area bent in the wind. Now sheets of rain blew across the asphalt. Mark squinted at the waiting cars. There had to be at least thirty cars, if not more, lined up to leave the island. Any one of them could be driven by smugglers.

He shook his head and sighed. "Let's start

checking each one. Look for anything suspicious. Maybe we'll get lucky."

Brock ran to the back of the line, and Mark turned toward the front. Rain dripped off his nose and chin, and he wiped it away. A chill prickled his skin. If he let those drugs get off the island, they would spread their poison into the lives of thousands of people. He couldn't let that happen.

He squared his shoulders and approached the first car.

FIFTEEN

Betsy strained against the ropes binding her hands behind her back, but it was no use. Her foolish decision to leave Treasury's had landed her in a terrible fix. At the moment, she lay tied and gagged in the hull of a boat transporting her to her death. Her clothes were soaked from the driving rain, but she knew from past experience the storm would only get worse. She would be left alone to drown in a concrete hole in a sandbar, and the only people who knew of her predicament were determined she would die. She suspected that would happen shortly.

The man at the controls of the boat cut the engine and glanced at his friend sitting beside him. "You need me to help you get her in the blind?"

He shook his head. "I think I can manage. Just be ready to get out of here. This rain is coming down harder, and I want to get back to shore."

He bent over, jerked her to her feet and threw

her over his shoulder like she weighed nothing. His muscles bulged under his shirt, and she squirmed to make carrying her more difficult. It didn't appear to bother him.

As if he was going for an afternoon stroll, he stepped out of the boat onto the submerged sandbar. Betsy could see the water lapping at his legs, and her heart dropped into her stomach. Usually when she came out to the curtain blinds, the water was only ankle deep. Now the water reached halfway to his knees.

He sloshed through the water to the curtain blind, shifted her from his shoulder, and dumped her into the blind. She gritted her teeth at the pain as she tumbled downward, her arms and legs scraping against the concrete sides of the box built to accommodate two standing hunters. When she hit the bottom, she tried to push to her feet but she couldn't. Her body lay wedged in the small enclosure.

The sound of splintering wood sent terror flooding through her. The man towered over the pit and hammered at the curtain surrounding the top of the enclosure. A silent scream welled up in Betsy's throat, but only a choking sound escaped her gagged mouth.

When he'd torn the complete curtain away, he glanced at the surrounding water and then leered down at her. "I guess that about does it, Miss

Michaels. The tide's getting higher. With no curtain to keep the water out, I don't think it'll be long before it'll all be over for you." He shook his head and directed a smirk in her direction. "You could have saved yourself a lot of trouble if you'd just done what we asked. Goodbye."

He disappeared from her sight, and Betsy listened to the boat motor grow faint in the distance. Hoping they would change their minds and return for her, she waited and listened but only heard the raging wind. She gazed upward and cringed at the jagged lightning streaks flashing across the sky. Claps of thunder shattered the air as the storm clouds moved closer to her watery prison.

The rain had already dumped several inches of water in the bottom of the blind, and Betsy knew she had to stand up. She wiggled around in the bottom of the concrete box until she was able to plant her feet on the bottom. Then, bracing her back against the wall, she slowly pushed up the side of the blind until she stood on her feet. Now able to see over the top, she stared at the water rising higher all around. At least she was able to see the storm that was growing more intense by the moment.

She didn't have time to celebrate her small victory before a huge wave poured over the sandbar and hit her full force. Gasping for air, she fell back to the bottom of the box into what now appeared to be several more inches of water. She lay there a moment trying to catch her breath, but instinct told her she had to get up. Better to die trying to find a way out than to lie still and wait for death.

Summoning all her strength, she pushed upright again until she could once more see the rising water. She spotted another wave headed her way and crouched below the rim of the box to avoid being hit. More water poured into the bottom and rose to her knees.

The water had soaked the cloth over her mouth, and she worked her jaw up and down in an effort to loosen the knot tied at the back of her head. She felt it slip a little. Bracing her head against the side of the blind, she rubbed the knot over the concrete until it loosened, and the gag slipped off her mouth. A few twitches with her chin and the cloth slid down to circle her neck.

She pushed to her feet once more, turned her face up to the drenching rain, and stared into the heavens. Rain pelted her, but she gazed upward. "God, I'm scared. Help me."

A memory of sitting beside her mother on the beach a few months before her death drifted into her mind. That day her mother had talked about dying and how she wasn't afraid. The words she'd spoken then drifted into Betsy's mind, and she could almost feel her mother's presence. *"I've trusted God all my life. Now I'm ready to trust Him after death."*

Her mother had known there was no hope left for her life just as Betsy knew she was about to die. Her chin quivered, and a tear rolled down her cheek. She looked up at the dark clouds, took a deep breath and offered up a prayer for God to watch over her family after she was gone.

Mark stopped at the back of the line of cars waiting to board the ferry. He'd walked by every one of them, and nothing had appeared out of the ordinary. Most of them contained families who were anxious about the coming storm and wanted to get to the mainland as soon as possible. His gaze drifted over the roofs of the cars barely visible now in the pouring rain. There had to be something he was missing. Drugs were hidden in one of those cars, but he had no idea which one.

Brock and Scott, wearing their yellow rain slickers, jogged from the front of the line and came to a stop beside him. Brock pulled his hat lower, and a stream of water poured to the ground. "Don't you want a rain suit?"

Mark shook his head. "It won't do any good now. I'm already soaked." He narrowed his eyes and stared at the waiting cars once more. "Those drugs are here somewhere. But where?"

"I don't know," Brock said. "I thought we might

see something suspicious right away. Since we haven't, we have to look further. I'll go tell the captain we aren't going to load until we complete a search of every car."

Mark groaned and rubbed the back of his neck. "That's going to take some time, and I hate to keep all these families here. But I don't see how it can be helped."

Brock nodded and turned toward the boat. "I'll be back to help. Go on and start with the first car and have Hamilton go from the back. Make sure nobody leaves until we're finished."

Scott nodded. "Will do." He turned to Mark. "Let's get started."

Mark followed Scott toward the front of the line. As he passed each car, he glanced inside. If only his gaze could penetrate metal, he could see where the drugs were hidden. Only action heroes could do that, and he was no hero. He'd thought he was a good agent, but he'd failed John Draper. If he had arrived a few minutes earlier at Springer's Point, John might still be alive, and Betsy might not have been put in harm's way.

He wiped the rain out of his eyes and wrinkled his brow as thoughts of that day at Springer's Point returned. Thanks to John's hard work, they now had the flash drive he'd downloaded and what appeared to be legitimate businesses would be raided within the next hours. His job on Ocracoke would be completed if he could find the drugs and arrest the smugglers.

He stopped at the first car and motioned for the man inside to roll down his window. The man frowned and complied. "Why are we being held up here? I'm in a hurry to get to Swan Quarter. I have an appointment this afternoon."

"I'm sorry, sir, but we're going to have to…" He stopped mid-sentence as his gaze locked on several wooden carvings in the backseat. He remembered seeing them in Luke's gallery when he'd been there.

The man frowned and glanced over his shoulder. "What's the matter?"

"Where did you get those carvings?"

"At Luke Butler's place. I like his work. I have a big collection of his decoys."

Decoys.

The word echoed in Mark's mind. What had John said to Betsy? He searched his mind before it came to him. *Tell him decoys not what they seem.*

What kind of message was John trying to send with his last breath? Betsy had told him she was calling the sheriff. Maybe he wanted her to tell them the smugglers would be able to fool them just like an unsuspecting duck who thinks he sees a friend bobbing on the water.

Mark thought back to the people he'd seen in the cars. Who would be the least likely to be accused of smuggling drugs? His gaze lit on an SUV about five car lengths back, and he knew.

"Scott," he yelled. "Come with me."

He clenched his fists and strode toward the vehicle. The window rolled down as soon as he stopped beside it. A smiling Miranda Walton greeted him. "Lizzy, look who's here. It's that nice young man we met. Can I help you?"

For a moment Mark couldn't speak. The two women cast puzzled looks at each other. Doubt whirled in his mind. How could two retired schoolteachers be smugglers? They were the least suspicious of anyone else in line. Exactly, he thought. Who would suspect two elderly women?

He took a deep breath. "Ladies, I'm afraid I'm going to have to ask you to get out of your car."

Miranda's eyes grew wide. "In this rain? Surely, you're not serious."

He nodded. "I am. We'll let you sit in one of the police cars while we search your vehicle. If everything checks out, we'll apologize and let you return."

Miranda's face grew red. "Sit in a police car?" she sputtered. "I can't do that."

Lizzy groaned and sank back against her seat. Her hand clutched at her chest. "Miranda, my medicine," she gasped. "I need it."

Miranda grabbed Lizzy's purse and fumbled inside of it. Mark reached in and took the purse from her hands. "Let me help." After a few minutes of searching, he looked up at Miranda. "There doesn't seem to be any medicine in here. We'll call the health center and have the EMTs transport her there to be checked out."

Lizzy took a deep breath and straightened. "That won't be necessary. I'm feeling better now."

The passenger door of the SUV opened, and Brock grasped Lizzy's arm. "Let me escort you to my squad car for now."

She cast one last glance in Miranda's direction before she climbed out and went with Brock. Miranda shrugged and stepped from the vehicle. Scott took her by the arm and followed Brock.

Deputy Hamilton ran up to Mark. "What do you want me to do?"

Mark pointed to the SUV. "I want us to tear this vehicle apart. Look in every possible place where drugs may be hidden."

The officer looked from Miranda and Lizzy getting into Brock's squad car and back to Mark. "You really think those two old ladies are smugglers?"

Mark took a deep breath. "I hope so, or I'm going to have a lot of explaining to do."

Thirty minutes later, Brock stood in front of the stripped-down SUV and directed the waiting cars to board the ferry. Mark walked to Scott's cruiser and stared at the bags of cocaine and two guns they'd found concealed inside the dashboard and under the seats of Miranda and Lizzy's vehicle.

Scott slammed the trunk shut and grinned. "You were right. Brock is sending our smugglers to the station with our other two guys. Are you ready to raid Will's studio?"

Mark nodded. "I am. Let's get this over with…I still haven't been able to reach Betsy."

Scott glanced up at the sky. "I'm really getting worried about her. Let's get this raid over with so we can find her."

Mark jumped into Scott's car, and they followed Brock through the rain-swollen village streets. Mark gripped the edge of his seat and swayed against the door as Scott turned a corner and headed to Will's studio. If everything went as they hoped, Will wouldn't have heard about the discovery at the ferry, and they could surprise whoever was present at the gallery.

The rain beat on the windshield and roof of the car. Mark checked his cell phone for messages again, but nothing new showed up. He swallowed the fear that gnawed at his stomach and stared out the window. Where was Betsy?

The water had risen to Betsy's waist, and it kept creeping higher. The rain now swept across the open water in sheets, and Betsy could see nothing but rolling waves and flashing lightning.

From time to time a wave would subside, and a flash of movement in the water several hundred yards away would catch her attention. She squinted and focused to determine if there was really something there or if her tired brain had conjured up the image.

A smaller wave rolled over the sandbar, and this time she saw it. The slatted, wooden wing where the blind's owner placed the decoys was anchored several hundred feet beyond the sandbar. Why hadn't she thought of it earlier? If she could get to it, she might be able to survive until someone found her.

Her spirits rose and crashed just as quickly. Her arms were tied behind her back, and another rope circled her ankles. *Think, Betsy. Find a way out of here.*

Her eyes grew wide as she remembered a night Scott had entertained their little sister, Emma, by showing her techniques he'd learned in the military. One of them was how to escape being tied up. But she was exhausted and had no idea if she could do what he'd shown them.

Once more she stared up at the sky. "Okay, God. I need You. Please help me to recall what Scott showed us."

Peace rolled through her soul, and she nodded. Backing up to one side of the blind, she slid down the concrete wall. When she reached the water level, she gulped in a big breath of air and continued her descent underwater until her hands touched her heels. Holding her breath, she tried to force her hands beneath her feet, but the rope snagged on the side of her shoe.

With her lungs about to explode, she pushed back above the water level. Taking two quick breaths, she plunged down into the water and tried again. This time her hands slipped all the way out from under her feet. Now her arms were tied in front of her.

She stood up, held her hands at face level and began to chew at the rope's knot. In minutes it loosened, and her wrists slipped free. She plunged back into the water and held her breath as she tugged to pull off the binding at her ankles. A newfound energy surged through her once she had kicked the rope aside.

Ignoring the water now flooding the concrete blind, she stared into the distance and waited for a flash of lightning. When it came, she spotted the wing's location. She grabbed the rim of the blind and pushed herself out of the box and into the water swirling over the sandbar. Now all she had to do was reach the curtain. Another streak of lightning lit the sky, and she saw the curtain bobbing in the water as if it beckoned her.

The water on the sandbar now came to her waist, but she waded as far as she could go before the small piece of land dropped off into the sea. She said one last prayer and plunged into the choppy sea. A wave washed over her and sent her spiraling downward and away from the sandbar. *God, help me.*

The water calmed for a few seconds, and she pushed upward. As she broke the surface, her head bumped against something. She stuck her hand up and grasped a wooden slate. She had reached the wing.

Grasping the sides of the wing, she pushed downward until she could lean her torso onto its surface. Slowly, she inched her way out of the water until she lay prone on the slatted platform.

A wave washed over her, and she tightened her grip to keep from being swept away. Chills raced through her body, and she fought against the exhaustion consuming her. All she wanted was to go to sleep, but she would slip into the water and drown if she drifted off.

Another wave hit full force, and she lost her grip. She slid toward the edge of the wing, her fingers searching frantically for a hold. Just before she slipped into the water, she grasped a slat with both hands and pulled herself back to the center of the wing.

Lightning flashed, and she buried her face against the back of her hands. If she could hold on until the storm subsided, maybe someone would

find her. Her fragile resting place bobbed in the water. *Don't let go. Hang on until help arrives.*
  She hoped help didn't come too late.

SIXTEEN

Thirty minutes later, with their prisoners locked in cells at headquarters, Brock and Scott pulled their squad cars to a stop in front of Will Cardwell's gallery. Mark had been on raids like this in the past, but you never knew what you might encounter once inside. Mark glanced around for Deputy Fisher who'd been watching the gallery and saw his squad car coast to a stop beside them.

They climbed out and closed the car doors quietly. No need to advertise their presence. Brock turned to Fisher. "Have you seen anything?"

He shook his head. "No movement at all."

"Good. That means they're still here. Hamilton is guarding the prisoners at the station, so it's just the four of us. You watch the door into the gallery. We'll go around to the studio entrance. When we have the situation stabilized inside, I'll call you in."

"Be careful," Fisher whispered.

"You, too," Mark said.

The three men drew their weapons and crept along the side of the building. They stopped at the corner of the gallery and flattened themselves against the wall. Brock peered around the corner. "A panel truck's at the back door. It looks like they're loading up to leave."

Mark leaned forward to catch a glimpse of what was going on but ducked back when a man carrying a box stepped outside and pushed it into the back of the truck. He nodded to Brock, and they stepped forward at one time and stuck their guns in the man's back.

"Get your hands up and move back inside slowly," Mark whispered.

The man froze for an instant before he glanced over his shoulder. He raised his hands and glared at them. "You're asking for trouble."

Brock pressed his gun into the small of the man's back. "You've already got it. Now move inside."

Mark's gaze darted about the room as they entered the studio where he'd watched Will teach would-be potters. Will looked up from bending over a box, and his face went white. "What's going on here?" he said.

Two men packing another box behind Will turned. Their eyes grew wide, and one reached for a gun lying on a table next to him. Mark stepped out from behind the man they'd encountered outside and held his gun in front of him. "I wouldn't do that. All of you, down on your knees and hands on your heads. You're all under arrest."

"You heard the man," Brock said. "You're under arrest for smuggling and the sale of illegal drugs." He turned his mouth to his lapel mic. "Situation stabilized."

He'd barely finished speaking before Deputy Fisher dashed in the back door with his gun drawn. Within seconds Will and his three cohorts had been cuffed and read their rights.

Rage mottled Will's face, and he glared at Mark as if he could kill him. When Scott pulled him to his feet, he lurched toward Mark, but Deputy Fisher and Scott restrained him. "So you're the one who took over for Draper. Too bad we didn't get you, too."

Mark stepped up to Will and stared into his eyes. "Yeah, too bad for you. I guess I was just lucky."

Will glanced over his shoulder at his men. "Did you hear that? He thinks he's lucky. Wouldn't it be nice if everybody was?"

Mark frowned. "What's that supposed to mean?"

Will cocked an eyebrow and directed a smirk at Mark. "Never mind. Let's go."

A feeling of doom surged through Mark, and he took a step back at the evil radiating from Will's eyes. A veiled threat had just been issued, but he had no idea who it was against. His heart hammered in his chest just as it had done the day he saw his parents' bodies in their car. He had to know what Will was talking about.

Will had insinuated someone hadn't escaped danger. But who? His heart skipped a beat, and his body turned cold as if the blood in his veins had suddenly frozen. His mind screamed her name over and over. *Betsy.*

He grabbed Will by the shirt and pulled him forward until their noses almost touched. "Where is she? What have you done with Betsy?" he yelled.

Will chuckled. "I think I'll lodge a complaint for police brutality."

Scott grabbed Mark's hands and pulled him loose. "Has he done something with Betsy?"

Mark shook his head. "I don't know."

And then he caught a glimpse of it lying on the floor underneath a table—flowers and butterflies in swirling bright colors. He scooped up the cell phone and held it up for Brock and Scott to see.

"This is Betsy's cell phone." He rushed at Will again, but Brock stopped him. "Where is she?" Mark cried out.

Will shrugged and looked away.

Scott looked as if he was in shock. He turned to Mark. "W-where do you think she could be?"

"There's no telling." His gaze swept across Will's hired men and came to rest on the youngest of the trio. He couldn't be more than nineteen or twenty years old, and he looked scared.

Mark grabbed the young man by the shirt and dragged him through the door that led into Will's gallery. He slammed the door behind him and took a deep breath. "Son, what's your name?"

"Andy."

"Well, Andy, you're headed to prison, and you have no idea what it's like to be locked up in a cage. I can already count enough charges against you to keep you there for years, but murder charges are a different matter. If Betsy Michaels dies, you'll be charged with her murder just like everybody else in the other room. You'll never see the outside world again in your lifetime."

Andy swallowed and tried to speak. "I—I ain't had nothing to do with murder. It was the others."

Mark felt as if a knife had just cut out his heart, but he couldn't let this prisoner see his fear. "It doesn't matter whether you did it or not—you'll still be held accountable if you have knowledge about it and don't tell me. If you help me, I'll talk to my superiors and see if we can't cut you a deal for a shorter sentence." He gritted his teeth and glared at Andy. "But if you don't, I'll see to it that you spend the rest of your life in prison. Is that what you want?"

"N-no."

"Then tell me."

Andy began to cry. Words spilled from his mouth, and the greatest fear Mark had ever known swelled up inside him. It was all he could do to keep from rushing into the other room and taking out his anger on Will Cardwell. That wouldn't do Betsy any good…and finding her was the most important thing at the moment.

When Andy had finished his story, Mark propelled him back into the studio and pushed him toward Brock. "Can you and your deputy take care of these guys? Scott and I have to go find Betsy."

Brock nodded. "Where is she?"

"In a curtain blind out on Pamlico Sound."

Scott's eyes mirrored the fear Mark felt. "My sister is in a curtain blind in this storm?"

"Yes. Let's get your boat and go find her."

They ran from the studio, jumped in Scott's squad car, and roared toward the marina where Scott kept his boat. Ten minutes later, with their life jackets securely fastened, they skimmed across the water of the harbor and out into Pamlico Sound.

As they sped toward the location of the curtain blinds, the storm intensified. Rain whipped him in the face, but Mark's thoughts centered on Betsy. According to Andy, Betsy had been left at the blind almost two hours ago. The storm surge had probably filled the concrete enclosure by this time. Was it possible that Betsy could survive in a storm like this?

Mark stared up at the sky and cringed at the lightning streaks. He had promised he would protect Betsy, and he hadn't. When he couldn't get Betsy on the phone earlier, he should have left to search for her. Brock and Scott could have handled the smugglers. His first priority should have been the woman he loved. He would never forgive himself for not saving her.

A loud clap of thunder startled him, and he jumped. He was helpless to do anything except look for Betsy right now. If she was still alive, though, he knew she wouldn't have given up. Her faith would have kept her fighting until the very end. He closed his eyes and prayed God would protect her until he could find her.

"Here's the first blind," Scott yelled.

He cut the motor and drifted closer to the spot where the first curtain blind was located. He pulled a flashlight from underneath his seat and swept the beam over the rolling water. There was no sign of Betsy.

After a few minutes of looking, Scott guided the boat away from the sandbar and headed toward the next one. The search there proved just as futile as the first stop. As they sped toward the next blind, the storm began to die down.

"The storm is moving toward the mainland," Scott shouted. "Maybe we can see better now." He pointed straight ahead. "Here's another blind."

Mark gripped the edge of the boat and swept the flashlight's beam across the water as they approached. "Betsy, it's Mark. Can you hear me?" he yelled.

Only the roar of the ocean answered.

He moved the light across the water again and stopped to focus it on something bobbing on the water's surface. "What's that?"

Scott peered in the direction of the light. "It looks like the wing of the blind."

"Can you get closer?"

Mark studied the wing as they approached. All at once his breath exploded from his mouth. "There she is!" he cried. "She's on top of the wing."

Before Scott could answer, Mark dived into the water and swam toward the wing. When he reached it, he didn't think he could touch her. What if he was too late and she was dead? He couldn't live knowing she was gone. With trembling hands, he grabbed Betsy's arm and shook it. "Betsy, it's Mark. Scott and I are here to get you."

She didn't move for a moment, and his heart dropped to the pit of his stomach. Then she raised her head and smiled. "I knew you would come. I hung on until you got here."

He pulled her toward him until she was at the edge of the wing, then wrapped his arms around her and pulled her into the water. Scott eased the boat up beside them and reached over the side to help lift Betsy into the boat. He laid her down and reached back to give Mark a hand.

Mark dropped down beside Betsy and swept her into his arms. All the way back to shore, he held her and thanked God for sparing her life. Just as Scott steered the boat into the harbor, she opened her eyes and gazed up at Mark. "You said you'd protect me, and you did. Thank you."

He wanted to speak, but he couldn't make his voice cooperate. He smiled and nodded. She closed her eyes and didn't speak again.

The EMTs, alerted by Scott of their arrival, waited onshore and whisked Betsy away to the health center as soon as they docked. When the ambulance carrying Betsy disappeared, Scott turned to Mark and stuck out his hand.

"Thank you for all you've done for my sister. I'll never be able to repay you."

Mark grasped his hand. "It was my pleasure. Betsy is the most wonderful woman I've ever met."

Scott cocked his head to one side and studied him. "I need to go to the station and help

Brock with our prisoners. I called Lisa, so all the Michaels women are headed to the health center right now. Are you ready to go see Brock?"

Mark debated where he should go before he responded. It was true he had a job to do, but tonight he had almost lost the most important person in his life. Nothing mattered more right now than seeing that Betsy was all right. He shook his head. "You and Brock can handle those guys. I'll wait at the health center to see what Doc has to say about Betsy."

Scott grinned. "Yeah, I think that's where you need to be, too. I'll drop you off on my way to the station."

Mark looked out the window of Scott's squad car as they drove to the health center. The storm had passed now, and large puddles of water filled the streets. They reminded him of the desperate minutes he and Scott had spent searching for Betsy. He closed his eyes and said a prayer of thanks to God for protecting her.

His time on Ocracoke had made him accept some important truths. He now understood what Betsy and Laura had meant when they spoke of their faith. There was still a lot about God and his newfound peace he needed to learn, but that would come with time.

Also, he'd faced the fact that he loved Betsy

Michaels. He probably had since he'd first known her, but his misguided vendetta for his parents' deaths had clouded his thinking. No matter how he felt, though, Betsy didn't return his feelings. He'd heard her tell her sister and sister-in-law he was the last man she would ever get involved with.

He didn't blame her for feeling that way. He had hurt her in the past, but he wouldn't anymore. The minute he knew she was out of danger, he would leave Ocracoke. He doubted if he would continue in police work, but he was sure God would be with him wherever he went.

In contrast to last night's storm, the morning sun streamed through the window at the health center. Betsy smiled and took a deep breath. It was great to be alive.

She glanced down at the outfit Kate had brought and helped her put on after Doc had agreed to let her go home. She patted her hair in place and waited for Mark to arrive. She remembered seeing him last night, but he hadn't yet come this morning. She wanted to thank him again for saving her life. But most of all, she wanted to tell him what she had promised herself she would do if she survived her terrifying ordeal. She was going to tell him she loved him.

It made no difference that he didn't love her.

She could live with that, but he deserved to know that he was worthy of love. She wanted him to remember that when he left Ocracoke.

A tap at the door startled her. She sat up straight in her chair and smiled. "Come in."

The door opened, and her heart plummeted. Scott hesitated before stepping into the room. "What's the matter? Aren't you glad to see me?"

She jumped up, ran to her brother and hugged him. "Of course I am. Why wouldn't I be after how you risked your life to save me?"

He shook his head. "Mark deserves most of the credit. He's the one who found your cell phone and forced one of Will's men to tell him what had happened to you. If it hadn't been for him, we might have been too late to rescue you."

"Then I'll have to thank him when he comes by. I thought he'd be here by now. I wonder what's keeping him." When Scott didn't answer her, she glanced at him. "What's the matter?"

Scott rubbed his neck and shook his head. "I don't know how to tell you this, but…"

"But what?" she interrupted.

He took a deep breath and exhaled. "Mark came by the office this morning to help us get our prisoners aboard the helicopter that took them to the mainland jail. After they left, he told Brock and me he was leaving today for Raleigh."

Betsy gasped and sank down on the bed. "Raleigh? Why would he leave without saying goodbye?"

"I don't know. He was like a wild man last night when we were looking for you. Then he sat in that chair by your bed all night. He didn't leave until Doc assured him you were going to be all right."

Tears streamed down Betsy's face. "But he can't go. I need to tell him how much I love him."

Scott grinned. "You do? Well, I have a hunch he loves you, too. Nobody goes as crazy as he did last night unless he's in love."

Betsy sprang up from the bed. "Do you really think he loves me?"

"I do." Scott glanced at his watch. "It's almost time for the ferry to leave. Why don't we try to stop him before he gets onboard?"

Betsy was out of the door and running down the hall before Scott could finish his sentence. They sprinted across the health center parking lot and jumped in Scott's squad car. "Turn on the siren, Scott. This is an emergency."

"You got it, sis," he said and pulled out into the street with his lights flashing and siren blaring.

Betsy grasped the edge of her seat as they sped to the ferry boarding area. As they approached, she saw cars lined up waiting to drive forward. She scanned the long line. "There he is, near the front."

Scott skidded to a stop, and Betsy jumped out. She ran to Mark's car and beat on the window. "Pull out of the line, Mark," she yelled.

The window rolled down, and Mark stared at her as if he couldn't believe his eyes. "Betsy, what are you doing here? You shouldn't be out of the hospital."

"Pull out of line, Mark. I need to talk to you."

He glanced at the cars in front of him that had begun to drive forward to the boarding ramp and back to her. "All right," he said and drove to the far side of the parking area.

She glanced back at Scott, who gave her a thumbs-up before she hurried over to Mark. When he got out of his car she stared up into his face. "Why are you leaving?"

The muscle in his jaw twitched, and he frowned. "I have a report to file and a case to finish up."

"Then what are you going to do?"

He raked his hand through his hair. "I don't know. Probably take some time off. I need to make some decisions about my life."

"Do those decisions have anything to do with me?"

"Yes." He swallowed. "Last night was the worst night of my life. I thought you were dead, and I didn't know how I could face that."

"Because you had promised to protect me?"

He nodded. "Partly, but most of all because of how I feel about you, Betsy." He took a step closer. "I know you still harbor a lot of anger at me over what happened in Memphis, and I don't blame you. But I love you. I can't be near you anymore without wanting to hold you in my arms, and it's killing me. I need to leave."

Her heart skittered in her chest, and she smiled. She reached up and caressed his cheek. "When I was hanging on to that wooden platform last night, I promised myself if I lived I would tell you how much I love you. I couldn't let you leave without telling you."

A look of wonder covered his face. "Do you really love me, Betsy?"

"I do, with all my heart. Please don't leave me."

She didn't know who made the first move, but suddenly they were locked in each other's arms. His lips covered hers, and her heart soared. He pulled back and stared into her eyes. "I can't believe this is happening."

She chuckled. "Oh, I can assure you it is." She pulled his head down, and they kissed again.

After a moment, he took a deep breath, held her at arm's length, and glanced over his shoulder at the cars that had started to board the ferry. "Betsy, I have to go to Raleigh and talk with my superiors. A lot has happened since yesterday, and we have to tie up all the loose ends. Maybe I can be back here in two weeks. Then we'll talk about when we're going to get married and where we're going to live." He paused and stared at her. "You will marry me, won't you?"

She laughed. "Of course I will, and I'll be right here waiting for you. You'd better call me every day, though."

His eyes grew wide. "I almost forgot." He reached in his pocket and pulled out her cell phone. "I meant to give this to Scott to return to you. Get it charged up so I can call you tonight."

"I will."

He kissed her once more and then laughed. "Who else would have a phone decorated with bright flowers and butterflies? I love you, Betsy Michaels."

"I love you, too, Mark Webber."

He jumped back in his car, and she watched as he drove onto the ferry. His car pulled on deck, and then he appeared at the railing. She stood in the boarding area and waved until the ferry disappeared out of the harbor and began its journey across Pamlico Sound to the mainland.

She glanced down at her cell phone and laughed. Bright flowers and fluttering butterflies, two of God's beautiful creations. And He had used that cell phone to bring Mark to her during the worst storm of the season. She breathed another prayer of thanks for bringing Mark into her life and walked back to where her brother waited. She could hardly wait to tell him they were about to have a new member in their family.

Three weeks later, Betsy and Mark sat on a blanket on the beach near Betsy's home. Her eleven-year-old sister, Emma, raced with Rascal, her beloved cat, along the water's edge. Betsy smiled in contentment. Mark had been back a week and they were already planning a Labor Day wedding.

She reached over and covered his hand with hers. "Happy?"

Smiling, he leaned over and kissed her. "I've never felt this good in my life. You're safe and well from your ordeal, and Will and his smugglers, along with two hired assassins disguised as elderly schoolteachers, are in jail where it looks like they'll be for a long time."

"I still can't believe Miranda and Lizzy were the ones who killed John."

"I can't, either, but the guns we found in their car matched the two bullets in John's body. They have quite a criminal background. They've worked for the drug cartel for years. There's no telling how many people they've killed. I get angry every time I think about how they helped orchestrate your abduction at the general store."

Her heart lurched at the memory. "I do, too."

"But thanks to John's flash drive, they won't be a threat any more. The DEA has closed down drug rings in four major cities." He leaned over and kissed her on the cheek. "Of course, the best thing that's happened is I'm going to marry the most beautiful woman in the world."

His words erased all the fears of the past weeks from her mind. She was safe now with the man she loved, and they had a lifetime ahead of them. The fact that he was devoted to her little sister only added to her happiness. "We have another blessing, too. Don't forget Mona. She's being released from the hospital tomorrow. That's some of the best news I've heard lately."

"Yeah, and my sister is going to come for our wedding before she moves to Memphis." He sighed. "I could go on forever thanking God for how everything turned out. How could life get any better?"

She grinned and gave him a playful punch on the shoulder. "It might get better if you had a job. I'm glad you decided to quit the DEA, but you need something to do."

He sat up straighter and nodded. "I agree. That's why I bought Luke Butler's studio this morning."

Her mouth dropped open and she gaped at him. "You did what?"

"Well, you know I've spent a lot of time over

there this past week. Luke kept talking about how he wanted to retire to the mainland. So I asked if he'd sell the building to me. I have a little money my parents left me, and it was enough to buy the place."

"B-but, you never said a word."

He wrapped his arm around her waist and pulled her closer. "I wanted to give you a surprise wedding present. I think it's time you had a larger place to work in than a room at Treasury's. There's enough space there for you to have your own studio, and I can have my workroom for carving. Then we can sell our work in the gallery showroom. What do you think?"

She shook her head in wonder. "I can't believe you bought Luke's gallery, but I'm thrilled." She put her arms around his neck. "I think that's the best present you could give me. But you may get tired of me being around all the time."

He gazed into her eyes. "I could never get tired of being with you. You've brought happiness back into my life, Betsy. I never thought that would happen. When I'm with you, I only think about things that make me happy." He pulled her closer. "Like flowers and butterflies."

"I want our lives to be filled with happiness. I love you so much, Mark. I'm going to spend the rest of my life showing you."

He drew her closer. "Those are the sweetest words I've ever heard." His voice was husky with emotion.

She closed her eyes and raised her lips to his. He was right. Life couldn't get any better than this.

* * * * *

Dear Reader,

Fatal Disclosure brings to an end the stories of the Michaels family members who live on Ocracoke Island. As I've written about the suspense and mystery that invaded the lives of Kate, Scott and Betsy, they have become as dear to me as the island where they live. In telling their stories, however, I've tried to show their faith in God and how they relied on His presence in their lives to face some dangerous situations. I hope you, too, have found the peace that comes from knowing God controls your life. The Bible tells us God will keep us in His perfect peace if our minds stay on Him. If you haven't found the everlasting strength He promises, I pray you will.

Sandra Robbins

Questions for Discussion

1. Betsy believed Mark had deceived her in the past. Have you ever had a friend who betrayed you? How did you react?

2. What does the Bible tell us to do when we believe a friend has wronged us?

3. How difficult is it for you to forgive a person for hurting you?

4. Mark's vendetta was caused by a traumatic experience in childhood. Are there memories from your childhood that still cause you pain? How do you deal with them?

5. Betsy knew Mark wasn't a believer, but she quit praying for him when she felt he had wronged her. What did Jesus say about praying for others?

6. Mark told Betsy one of the things he admired about her was that she saw the good in other people. Do you look for the good in others even when you think they don't deserve it?

7. Mark overheard Betsy's hurtful words to her sister and sister-in-law about him. Have you

ever spoken words that hurt or offended another person? What should we do when that happens?

8. Laura lost her parents and her fiancé to violence. Have you experienced the loss of someone you love through an act of violence? How have you coped with your loss?

9. Mona felt trapped in an abusive relationship with her boyfriend. Have you in the past or at present suffered abuse in a relationship? What steps did you take or are you taking to remove yourself from that environment?

10. Betsy's impulsive nature led her into trouble even after she had been warned. Do you ever act before you think? How can you break that habit?

11. When Betsy thought she was dying, she remembered how her mother faced death, and it gave her the peace to put her situation in God's hands. Do you show your children a strong faith in God every day? If not, what do you need to do to change how your children perceive you?

12. Mark and Betsy each had a God-given talent. What gift has God given you? How are you using it to glorify him?

LARGER-PRINT BOOKS!

**GET 2 FREE
LARGER-PRINT NOVELS
PLUS 2 FREE
MYSTERY GIFTS**

Love Inspired®

SUSPENSE
RIVETING INSPIRATIONAL ROMANCE

Larger-print novels are now available...

LISUSLP11B

LARGER-PRINT BOOKS!

GET 2 FREE
LARGER-PRINT NOVELS
PLUS 2 FREE
MYSTERY GIFTS

Larger-print novels are now available...

YES! Please send me 2 FREE LARGER-PRINT Love Inspired® novels and my 2 FREE mystery gifts (gifts are worth about $10). After receiving them, if I don't wish to receive any more books, I can return the shipping statement marked "cancel". If I don't cancel, I will receive 6 brand-new novels every month and be billed just $4.99 per book in the U.S. or $5.49 per book in Canada. That's a saving of at least 23% off the cover price. It's quite a bargain! Shipping and handling is just 50¢ per book in the U.S. and 75¢ per book in Canada.* I understand that accepting the 2 free books and gifts places me under no obligation to buy anything. I can always return a shipment and cancel at any time. Even if I never buy another book, the two free books and gifts are mine to keep forever.

122/322 IDN FEG3

Name	(PLEASE PRINT)

Address	Apt. #

City	State/Prov.	Zip/Postal Code

Signature (if under 18, a parent or guardian must sign)

Mail to the **Reader Service:**
IN U.S.A.: P.O. Box 1867, Buffalo, NY 14240-1867
IN CANADA: P.O. Box 609, Fort Erie, Ontario L2A 5X3

Not valid to current subscribers to Love Inspired Larger-Print books.

**Are you a current subscriber to Love Inspired books
and want to receive the larger-print edition?
Call 1-800-873-8635 or visit www.ReaderService.com.**

* Terms and prices subject to change without notice. Prices do not include applicable taxes. Sales tax applicable in N.Y. Canadian residents will be charged applicable taxes. Offer not valid in Quebec. This offer is limited to one order per household. All orders subject to credit approval. Credit or debit balances in a customer's account(s) may be offset by any other outstanding balance owed by or to the customer. Please allow 4 to 6 weeks for delivery. Offer available while quantities last.

LILP11B